The Hartwood Inheritance

JUNE FAIRFIELD

This is a fiction novel. All events and characters expressed are from the author's own imagination. Any relation to real life people or places is coincidental.

For my husband–

Thank you for the never-ending encouragement, support, and love.

Chapter One:

An Evening at Hartwood

The carriage had scarcely cleared the gravel drive of Ashcombe Park before Father began tapping his cane lightly against the floor, a habit he always denied yet never quite seemed to stop.

"You'll do very well tonight, my girl," he said benevolently. "Aunt Charlotte always gathers an excellent crowd for her balls."

"She certainly does," I replied, watching the hedgerows pass. "Though excellent crowds always seem to require such excellent effort."

He gave a short laugh. "Effort is the currency of society, Bridget. You cannot expect to receive without spending a little of yourself."

I sighed as I twisted my sash around in my hand.

"Or a lot of yourself," I muttered. "Why must I purchase anything?"

"Because security, comfort, and good standing are things not given for free," Mother interjected, slightly annoyed at having to explain this yet again. "And if you would put forth an effort to sit up straight, you might also purchase a respectable impression."

She began to fuss at my appearance as she straightened the lace cuff on my sleeve, wiped a smudge off my shoe, and tucked in the loose curl of auburn hair that always seemed to fall across my forehead.

Father's eyes flicked toward me, amused. "Your mother is right. A young lady cannot linger forever in observation. You must join in on the conversation, take part in the splendor of forming connections with others."

"I do not *linger*," I said quietly. "I simply like to understand things before I participate."

Mother gave a disapproving look as Father looked at me intently, and his expression softened. "Let her be, Rosamund. She observes before she acts. There are worse habits."

This comment earned him a stern glance from Mother. The defense was gentle, but it warmed me all the same.

"You will dance tonight," he said, turning back to me, an attempt to appease Mother, no doubt. "If only once. For my sake."

"For yours?" I asked, surprised.

"For mine," he said, though his smile came a moment too late. Something in his tone gave me pause. I studied him more carefully, the way his jaw seemed to clench whenever his thoughts drifted from the present moment, the way his eyes almost seemed to cast a shadow behind them, the restless energy he could not quite contain.

"You are uneasy," I said quietly.

He let out a breath that might have been a laugh. "My perceptive daughter."

The carriage had slowed to a stop, reaching its impending destination. Mother was the first to step out, and when she wasn't looking, Father untucked the curl from my hair and let it cascade across my forehead and resume its usual position.

"Remember, child, seeing clearly is a gift; do not give it up just to appease those around you," he said.

I almost asked him why he had been so burdened lately, sensing there was more beneath his thoughtful demeanor. His quiet tension made me feel worried, and I longed to understand what was the matter, but the moment passed all too soon as he briskly left the carriage.

The ballroom of The Hartwood Estate had always been the grandest place I had ever been, but tonight it felt especially extravagant. Aunt Charlotte had gone to extraordinary lengths to ensure not even a single flower was out of place. I almost felt dizzy at the general movement of shiny silks and sparkling jewels. The symphonic sound of polite laughter and forced pleasantries caused me to feel unpleasant. I moved through it, however, as if I were an actress in a play, my face a happy misrepresentation of the dreadful boredom I felt within. Mother would be so proud of my near-scripted conversations filled with nothing but compliments and inquiries. The echo of my Father's words reverberated in my mind more prominently than the music did: "Seeing clearly is a gift." I did not always view my observations in the same light, and often wished this so-called gift had been bestowed on someone else. It made these events intolerable. I detested noticing how Mrs. Penbury's feathers in her frizzy hair made her head look like a giant pheasant was sitting atop it. And how Lord Beuford was on his fifth glass of wine and acting a little too comfortable around the young Miss Isabelle, or how my father, Lord James Richard Hartwood, had been absent from the room for almost the entirety of the evening.

Just when I was about to attempt an escape out to the gardens, I saw him. William Finch. A mixture of relief and something akin to confusion shot through me. He was handsome, always had been, and the whispered possibility of a future with him had occupied my thoughts more than I cared to admit.

I allowed one of my earliest memories of William to drift to the forefront of my mind, and with it, a warm smile rose across my face. We were both much younger and were indulging in the general frivolity most children do at such an age, as we were running through the corridors of Ashcombe Park, even after being instructed not to. In my haste, I had lost my balance around a corner and collided rather unfortunately into one of Mother's favorite vases. The sound shattered through the building, followed by a dreadful silence. William caught up to me only to find me in tears. Not long after him, our parents arrived to see what the matter was. Before I could think up the words for an explanation, William stepped forward.

"It was me," he had said simply. "We were chasing one another down the hall when I collided with the vase. I am truly sorry, Mrs. Hartwood. It shan't happen again."

The reprimand that followed suit was entirely undeserved, but he seemed to bear it almost happily. Afterwards, I inquired why he so willingly took the blame for my wrongdoing, to which he had replied, "I couldn't bear to see you in further pain, Bridget."

Ever since then, he has always been there, willing and ready to soften whatever roughness I accidentally, or not quite so accidentally, bring into the world.

I have come to recognize several of his most common habits over the years, such as clearing his throat and pulling at his cuff when he feels nervous or uncomfortable. And when something sincerely amuses him, not the polite laughter society demands, his eyes crinkle at the corners, and he ducks his head, as though embarrassed by the feeling itself. He is steady where I am impulsive, thoughtful where I am outspoken.

I was lulled out of my silent reverie when I overheard someone nearby speak his name. "Ah, yes, that's William Finch. I heard not a few moments ago from Mrs. Lowell that Miss Isabelle, daughter of Lord and Lady York, has taken a real interest in him. And why should she not? He is quite a charming young lad, and with her family's fortune, she stands in the rare position to be able to marry whomever she wants, of good standing that is."

My heart felt as though it had dropped from my chest to the floor. Miss Isabelle, interested in William? *My* William? His family was not of noble blood, but his father, Augustus, was an extremely successful banker and financier, and was rather popular at parties; he had somehow managed to insert himself into high society decades ago. Surely his brotherly friendship with my father assisted in that matter.

But Miss Isabelle? The thought made my stomach begin to churn. I begrudgingly had to admit she was a beauty, what with her blonde hair, almost always adorned with eccentric jewels, and her petite frame, which made her seem more delicate than most. She was, without a doubt, the most sought-after young lady by gentlemen of many ages, and she had set her sights on William.

I dared a slight glance in his direction. He stood among the guests, as he always did, well-dressed, composed, the picture of quiet confidence, his brown hair catching the light, his handsome stature unmistakable. He had always been popular and comfortable in a crowd.

When our eyes met, his smile came a moment too late, and though it was warm, it did not quite reach his eyes as it usually did. It seemed as if he was about to leave his current conversation to head towards me when I saw Miss Isabelle approach him, whisper something in his ear, and grab his arm. He smiled politely, and they made their way to the dance floor.

I felt my ears burn with envy. Of course, William had danced with plenty of other girls before, but I couldn't help but feel him slipping out of my reach this time. After all, why would he not want to position himself handsomely within a marriage to a wealthy woman? Not that he wanted for money, his father had been training him in the financial business, but the prospect of even more money tends to make people behave in a way they wouldn't ordinarily behave.

The past few months have been uncharacteristic of our amicable relationship. William began to pull away, avoid me in town, and ignore my letters, all the while offering me no explanation. The change struck me now with a bitterness that felt entirely out of place amid the light and frivolity surrounding us. No doubt, this potential engagement was the cause of his estrangement.

The song ended, and I unhappily observed him and Miss Isabelle bow and smile at each other, both winded and cheeks aglow from the lively dance. It was not long after that that he and I exchanged another glance across the room as I was conversing with a portly gentleman whose name I could hardly remember. I looked away but felt his brown-eyed gaze linger on me. Not long after, he requested the next dance. I obliged with little enthusiasm. He took my hand and led the way. I fought to hide my disappointment. His hand found my waist; the familiar warmth was there, but the usual easy banter was absent, replaced by a stilted politeness that irked me.

“Quite a lovely night for a ball, don't you agree?" He posed. We rarely engaged in common pleasantries like this, often just getting to the point we wished to convey.

"Quite lovely indeed, Lady Charlotte outdid herself as usual," I replied. I was not about to let him see how much his stiff politeness was straining my patience as we continued in the slow cotillion dance, and our conversation was interrupted as we swapped partners, then once again returned to one another.

"Bridget," he stated, his voice lower than usual.

I braced myself for an informative comment about how he would be making an offer of marriage to Miss Isabelle tonight. I planned to show little interest in the news.

But then he continued quietly, “You must keep your distance from your father.”

The words sent confusion through me, jarring me from my carefully constructed composure.

"Keep my distance?" I rebuttled, my own voice betraying me with a tremor of anger and hurt. The pattern of the dance separated us once more, and I felt my body move by memory, not by will.

Our hands reunited, and he continued, "Yes, I cannot explain why, but you must promise me you will do this. You have to trust me."

My disbelief was overshadowed only by my hurt.

"So I am expected to simply just carry on without you, and now my father as well? Whom else shall I shun from my life?" I said, unable to mask my hurt.

The music filled the room around us as we continued to go through the motions of the dance; however, nothing else seemed to exist except for the sudden storm brewing between us.

"Bridget," he sounded pained, "I just want you to be safe, please."

The dance concluded in that moment, our eyes met briefly as we bowed, a chasm of unspoken words separating us. He reached his hand out towards me, as if to explain further, then lowered it quickly, pursing his lips as if he was making a real effort to keep himself from speaking more. I excused myself to seek the fleeting solace of a drink as my head swirled with frustration and sorrow. He just wants me to be safe? Safe from my own father? What an odd thing to say.

It was then, as I sipped my glass trying to cool the growing rage within me, that I beheld the most peculiar sight. It was Father's cousin, whom I affectionately referred to as cousin as well, Lord Rupert Hartwood. His face appeared weary from exertion as he ran with as much haste as his senile legs would allow towards the front entrance of the estate. The sight was such a surprise that my heart seemed to beat at the increased speed of his steps, and I felt as if I could not move as fast as I intended. Rupert was followed not far behind by his mother, Charlotte, whose usual composure seemed shattered by unmistakable terror. I wove through the crowd without a second thought, lured in by whatever drama was unfolding outside the home in the stark embrace of night. A chill began to move its way down my spine.

I walked through the open doors and found several people surrounding someone lying still, too still, at the bottom of the grand stairs. Great Aunt Charlotte's sobs struck my heart like a whip on a horse.

As I reached the small crowd, I lost my own composure when I recognized the body as that of my father's; at his side lay shards of a shattered wine glass, glinting in the dim lantern light. Upon inspection, the scene immediately answered what had happened to him: he had indulged a bit too much in alcohol, something he often did, misstepped on his way back into the party, and fell down the many stairs to a fatal landing. It was a tragedy, stark and undeniably real. I felt frozen in place.

Aunt Charlotte's words, "Your father, he is dead," repeated over and over in my mind.

My mother was not too far behind me; her panic and tears quickly joined in with mine and Aunt Charlotte's. Grief began to cloud my mind; the world seemed to tilt unnaturally as I knelt on the ground in grand disbelief, my thoughts stubbornly ringing one question over and over: what had compelled William to warn me away from my father on the same night of his death?

Chapter Two:

Generosity

The subsequent hours were filled with hushed tones and the slow departure of guests bidding mournful regrets, all walking and talking carefully, as if they too were about to fall down the grand staircase. No one would quite meet my eye, except for William. He gently took my hand in his; his grip firm and warm. His eyes searched mine, and I felt a great sorrow exude from his countenance that made my throat constrict.

"Bridget… I am so immeasurably sorry," he declared with restraint and weariness, as if the words he spoke might break his steady composure. There was no grandeur in the way he spoke, only sincerity.

A glint from the area where Father's body had been found drew my attention, and my gaze momentarily locked onto the shattered wine bottle left behind, its broken glass shining like a fragment of the night's chaos. Suddenly, the memory of Mother's vase I broke as a child, the one William had taken the blame for, flickered across my mind. For the briefest moment, I longed for him to step forward, shoulder this burden, somehow take the pain of this tragedy away from me, just as he had so many a time before with so many now seemingly meaningless things. But death was not a broken vase, and no one could take the pain of grief away. No, not even William, especially not him. Not after his vague and cryptic warning just moments before the accident that now seemed to cast a shadow over an already dark evening.

An oppressive quiet settled over the house as each carriage took its leave, and the grand estate that had been full of life and music and laughter only hours ago now seemed colder, darker, and shadowed by an unspoken grief that lingered like a heavy fog.

Mother and I remained in Charlotte's drawing room long after the last condolences had been offered. The time passed with little reprieve, and at some late hour we had sunk together upon the sofa, still adorned in our ball gowns, still clutching one another, and slept there like children who had stayed up long past their bedtime. When I awoke, my neck ached, and the fire had burned low, but Mother's hand was still wrapped tightly in mine, as though she feared that letting go might mean she would lose me too.

The thought came and would not leave me: how were we ever to return to Ashcombe Park? It had been our home, the setting for my childhood, each room a witness to the life I had lived up until this point. But alas, Father was gone now, and took with him the illusion of security we so happily were engaged in. I knew, even in my deep sorrow, what his death meant for Mother and me. There would be arrangements, changes, and the home I had left only last night had now slipped beyond our reach and would pass into the possession of some distant relative we knew nothing about.

Aunt Charlotte was three steps ahead of us as usual, though. "What a tragedy, my dears," she had said last night once the final guest had left. "If I have any say in the matter, I must insist that you avoid destitution. Ashcombe Park very well shall pass into another's hands, but this is the Hartwood Estate, and you are both Hartwoods. So here you shall reside. The cottage near the main house will be quite comfortable, suitable enough to mourn this great loss away from prying eyes and ears, yet close enough for me to ensure you are well taken care of. And you may dine with Rupert and me as often as possible. I shall not have you sitting alone, fretting yourselves into illness."

"Oh, Charlotte, we couldn't possibly," Mother started.

But Charlotte only raised her hand and countered, "I really must insist. We have more than enough to care for the cottage; you can keep a couple of your staff on from Ashcombe Park. It will be a smaller life, but a safe and comfortable one nonetheless, while you can sort through this mess."

Mother attempted a weak protest as Charlotte lovingly grabbed her hand before she could even utter another word.

"No," she said gently. "I shall not accept any rejection of my generosity, dear. You are in need, and I am in surplus. You will stay here, and that is the end of it."

Aunt Charlotte's capacity for compassion shone through more brightly than usual in this circumstance, no doubt due in large part to her own experience with widowhood; it seemed she knew exactly what my mother needed and effortlessly anticipated her needs.

We were untethered now, cast loose from everything familiar. And yet, in that moment, Charlotte's generosity gave us somewhere to land. She was, after all, the widow of the great Lord Richard Hartwood, who many years ago had passed away from Tuberculosis. His immense fortune had passed to his son, Rupert, and enabled the continuation of extravagant living, coordinated entirely by Charlotte.

Allowing us to live on the estate would hardly be an inconvenience for them.

I finally rose from the couch, intending to make my leave and gain some fresh air. I smoothed the creases from my gown as best I could, but almost any attempt to erase the effects of the previous night seemed to be in vain. The drawing room was quiet, bathed in the soft glow of morning. Someone, one of Charlotte's staff, no doubt, had drawn back the curtains and set a tray of tea and bread on the table near us. The house, it seemed, had resumed its usual order without us.

I stepped outside the door to find that the day was incredibly bright. Sunlight fell warm across the lawns as a light breeze rustled the surrounding trees. Birds were chirping joyfully, flying freely from tree to tree with nothing to hold them in one solitary place. I envied them. It was a strange cruelty, how everything remained so beautifully composed out here after the horror of the night before.

I wandered along one of the pristine, immaculately maintained gravel paths, hardly noticing where I was heading, my thoughts heavy and unformed. Why had William been so perplexing? And why did his distance from me seem to occur at the same time father's countenance had grown wearier and wearier these past months? I must have turned a corner too quickly because my foot collided with something solid, a stone perhaps, and I stumbled forward with a small cry. A pair of steady hands caught me before I reached the ground.

"Beg pardon, miss," a voice said at once, alarmed and earnest, with a hint of a foreign accent behind it. "I should have kept clearer of the path."

The stranger assisted me back to my feet, and as I looked up, I was startled to find a young man beside the flowerbed he had been obviously tending to. A glance at his clothes left no doubt that he was one of Aunt Charlotte's many groundskeepers, for she had many. His gloved hands covered in soil, a fact he seemed to remember as he released my arm at once, and bowed his head respectfully.

"I hopc you are not hurt."

"No, no, I am quite well," I said, though my heart was still racing. "It was my own clumsiness."

He offered a faint, apologetic smile. I couldn't help but notice his olive-toned skin glinting with sweat from his labors. His gaze softened as it lingered on my face.

"You've been crying," he said gently, not as a question but as a quiet observation. A slight pause entered between us.

"I heard what happened last night," he added, "I am very sorry, miss." The words were simple, spoken without curiosity or intrusion, only sympathy. Something in his tone, steady and sincere, caught me off guard. I nodded, feeling heat rise into my cheeks.

"Thank you," I managed at last.

He inclined his head again, as though the matter required no further attention, and returned his hands rather quickly to the earth beside him, careful and deliberate in his work. There was a uniquely calm presence about him that lingered even as the morning stretched bright and indifferent around us. I could not help but feel a little awkward for interrupting his morning's work, and began to make my leave when another manly voice cut through the quiet.

"Excellent job over here, boss says we are to head over to the west wing of the home now; there are some unruly shrubs that require pruning."

Another groundskeeper, clearly sent to fetch this other worker, noticed me as he turned to leave. "A thousand pardons, miss, I did not see you there. Come along, Antonio, let's leave the Lady in peace."

Antonio looked down at the flowerbed he had been weeding, as if he were reluctant to leave a job unfinished, but rose quickly. He cast a fleeting, almost apologetic look my way before leaving the area.

Once they were gone, I shook my head quickly, noticing that this stranger's rugged charm and earnest demeanor left an impression on me that, for a moment, caused me to forget my own despair. I allowed myself to ponder a moment more on his slightly long dark hair and deep green eyes, but the quiet of the morning resumed almost instantly, and, alone again, I sank onto a nearby stone bench. The surrounding roses began to feel stifling. The events of the past night, my father's sudden demise, pressed down on me, and tears once again coursed down my cheeks. I must have been crying for nearly an hour or so, because I began to feel the sun burn my skin as it rose higher in the sky. I brushed away the stray curl that had fallen onto my face yet again, then noticed something catch the sunlight near my feet.

Curiosity drew me in as I picked up the object, which happened to be a rather thick shard of glass. The jagged piece bore an image resembling part of an animal, perhaps a lion. Upon further inspection, I noticed a dark, ominous stain on one edge. Blood. I felt chills run up and down my back as I recalled the shattered glass near my father's body just the night before. Did this belong to the same bottle found near his corpse? If so, why was it so far from the debris near where Father was found? I felt my heart begin to beat at a quickened pace, and sweat began to wet my forehead. The sun's heat, combined with this peculiar discovery, made me apprehensive. I stood up to return to the house. Mother would not approve of my face turning red from the sun. I stuffed the shard into the sleeve of my dress, intending to inspect it further later on.

I returned to find Mother resting on the sofa where I had left her, her eyes open now but distant, as if someone had placed a thick pane of glass in front of her, preventing her from seeing through it. She noticed my presence as I rejoined her, and she reached for my hand in absolute silence. I sat beside her, and together we endured the morning in a quiet that felt heavier than any sadness uttered aloud.

The day passed slowly and grimly as voices were kept low, and every movement in the house seemed to tiptoe around us awkwardly. It was difficult to believe that only hours before, the halls had been full of music and laughter.

The despair seemed to come and go in waves. Mother would frequently put her head in her hands and cry, "James… oh, James, what have you done?" And I cried with her. There were no words that seemed possible to console the heart of a wife recently turned widow, and a daughter recently turned fatherless.

Aunt Charlotte, dear Aunt Charlotte, had stayed true to her word. And in her nurturing manner, she was taking care of everything. Not only had she already begun arrangements for the funeral, but she had sent staff to Ashcombe Park to pack up our things and close the house. There was no telling when, or if, we would be able to return.

Mother mustered all the strength she could to sojourn the short walk along a charming path to the small cottage on Aunt Charlotte's estate.

The cottage was made of brick and appeared to be tucked comfortably among a grove of trees. The quaint edifice held itself in a peaceful, quiet way. Charlotte was right; it seemed the perfect place to mourn. The cottage had been used many a time in the past as a place for guests when the main home did not have enough space, an issue so rarely run into due to the enormity of the home. I took a few deep breaths, taking in our new humble refuge. When we arrived, the place was buzzing with servants and maids who were quickly pulling sheets off furniture, starting the fire, and warming a pot of tea on the stove. I felt the coldness of the shard of glass as it pressed against my arm, hidden in my sleeve. I yearned to pull it out to examine it further, but there wasn't a single solitary place to allow me to do so, so I waited and tried to push the shard from my mind.

"My Lady," began Mr. Smith, our Butler from Ashcombe Park, who was designated to remain in our service thanks to the generosity of Aunt Charlotte, "Please come to the front room while the staff sees to the bedrooms. You shall be quite comfortable there."

It was refreshing to sec a familiar face. Mr. Smith had been with our family for decades now, and I had known him my entire life. His loyalty towards our family felt genuine, and I had always loved the way he smelled of chamomile.

"This way now," he encouraged Mother to move. It felt as if she was still in shock. He offered her his arm and guided her to a chair near the fireplace. "Do try to relax, madam, you've been through a wretched ordeal. I will be back with your tea," and with that, Mr. Smith left the room.

Mother sat in the chair near the fireplace; it was as if she could not move or speak unless someone encouraged her to. Our things, recently brought in from Ashcombe Park, were scattered around the place as the staff attempted to establish a proper order. In the crowded room full of people shuffling in and out, I noticed a small box of mine, where I had stored letters William had written me over the years. Hoping no one had opened the box, I took it quickly, sank into the sofa in the front room, and removed the lid to find the rather large stack of letters. I pulled one out at random and opened it, seeking some measure of consolation. It was one I had read over and over many a time, even though William had written it to me only last year. I smiled at the consolation of this particular memory.

Dear Bridget,

I must write to you regarding a most cruel injustice. It has been brought to my knowledge, by my mother no doubt, that I have behaved with impeccable rudeness at Charlotte's dinner party last night by laughing when you compared Mr. Hardwick's new coat to a circus tent. After all, Mr. Hardwick was not present, and you were merely stating a fact, and did so with such admirability.

Still, I have been told that a gentleman ought not to encourage such observations. If that is true, then I fear I have been a poor gentleman for many years now, for encouraging you has always brought me great pleasure.

You will be pleased to know that Colin suggests you to be the most dangerous conversationalist in Ashcombe. His reasoning is that you are able to speak what others are thinking in a way that remains charming. I dare say he is quite accurate in this statement, though I would never give him the satisfaction of being correct about anything.

In any case, I expect to see you soon, if only so that I may encourage your free speech all the more.

Until then,

William

I sighed as I pictured him stifling a laugh as best he could after I had said something Mother would deem utterly ridiculous. He had always been a loyal accomplice in mischief, and his company was one I longed for the most. I felt comfortable in his presence, which is something I could not say of most other eligible bachelors. It had been a great challenge for me to open up to other gentlemen at the many societal events Mother had us attend. I always felt out of sorts and pressured, like I would be expected to marry a man after having only danced with him once. Oh, how I wished William were here now. I held back tears as I felt the loss not only of Father, but of William too. I now had to somehow live my life without both of them.

As evening drew on, the activity within the cottage faded, and the house settled into a hush that felt almost unnatural after the long day. The cottage stood in stark contrast to the grandeur of Ashcombe Park, yet it still had a sense of home.

"M'lady? Shall I help you prepare for bed?" Jane asked softly. She was the one maid we had been able to keep on, a capable girl. Outspoken at times, but steady and efficient when it mattered most.

“I suppose I ought to,” Mother said, her voice worn and unsteady from hours of weeping.

“I’ll return for you shortly, Miss Bridget,” Jane added before guiding Mother down the hall.

I was alone once more. I drew the shard of glass from my sleeve and turned it slowly in my hand. In the firelight, it caught and scattered the glow, bending it into a dull, distorted blur. Nothing appeared as it truly was through that thick, broken edge—only a warped shimmer of what truly was, much like my thoughts. I stared into the fractured light, my thoughts drifting between grief and doubt, until exhaustion pressed in and the night settled heavily about me.

Chapter Three:

My Gift

I awoke the next morning to find myself staring at an unfamiliar ceiling. The disorientation began to fade slowly but surely as I peered around to find the morning's light settling about the room. The bed beneath me was smaller and lumpier than the one at Ashcombe Park. The air faintly smelt of burning firewood and freshly baked bread. My memory began to return heavily, like a door creaking open on its hinges.

The cottage.

Father was gone. Ashcombe Park was no longer ours to return to. And this—this small, orderly room—was to be home now, at least for a time.

I turned onto my side and drew the cover closer, feeling the dull weight of exhaustion settle again into my limbs as I recalled how I ended up in this bed. Jane had woken me by the fire the night before and had kindly guided me up the stairs and into this room. She had helped me wash, change out of my blue gown, and coaxed me into bed as if I were a child again. She spoke the whole time reassuringly; she was never at a loss for words and could often fill a quiet room with conversation all on her own. "It'll get easier with each passing day, m'lady, you'll see," she had said.

I had slept far later than I meant to. The sun stood well above the trees now, its light casting a warmth on the world that seemed capable of reaching everything but me. Things didn't feel easier, not yet.

My gaze drifted toward the vanity. There, exactly where I had left it, lay the shard of dark glass, its jagged edge shining in the morning light. It was almost as if the shard was trying to stand out as much as it possibly could in an effort to tell me something.

"Shall I dispose of it, miss?" Jane had asked, holding it carefully between her fingers.

"No," I had said at once, too quickly, perhaps. "No… just leave it there."

She had done so without question, placing it neatly upon the vanity and turning her attention back to the laces on my dress. I trusted Jane. I always had. She had been with us not as long as other staff had, but long enough to know my moods, my faults, the small rebellions of my nature. I had spoken to her freely of my frustrations with Mother, my uncertainties about society, even of my foolish hopes where certain gentlemen were concerned.

But this, this was different. I could not confide in her in this matter. I was still attempting to accept the strange thought prevailing over my mind, the thought that Father perhaps did not simply fall during a drunken stupor. Perhaps, there were other forces at play here, perhaps something more nefarious had claimed his life instead. I attempted to push this thought from the forefront of my mind; naming it out loud would make it feel all too real, and I was not certain I was ready for that. So the shard remained there atop my vanity, silent and waiting, bathing in the morning light as I attempted to make sense of the new life I had ahead of me.

By the time I dressed and made my way downstairs, the cottage had settled into the subdued quiet of a house harboring mourners. Breakfast was laid upon the table in the small dining room—tea, bread, a dish of preserves neither of us would touch—and Mother sat already at the table, her hands folded in her lap as though she had forgotten what they were meant to do. She looked smaller there, her figure diminished, her posture stooped, and her face drawn with exhaustion, as if the weight of grief had pressed into her very bones.

"You have slept late," she pointed out.

"Yes, I suppose I needed the rest," I replied as I sat in the chair across from her.

We ate very little; the only sound in the room was the small clink of china as we sipped our morning tea, our feeble attempt at normality requiring more effort than either of us seemed to possess. Jane entered the room quietly and began pouring us more tea, her usual briskness softened by sympathy.

Mother stared down into her cup for a long moment before speaking again.

"It is such a senseless thing," she murmured, her voice unsteady. "To die in such a foolish manner. Drinking himself into such a state and then slipping down the stairs."

The words landed heavily between us. I felt something tighten in my chest, a sharpness, an insistent anger almost, that was entirely unwelcome. The image of the shattered bottle rose at once in my mind, yet again. Why had I found it where it did not seem to belong?

Father had never cared for wine; Brandy had always been his tipple of choice, and yet there it was, a shattered wine bottle beside him.

"It seems almost impossible," Mother spoke faintly, "To lose everything so quickly."

I pressed my hands together beneath the table, feeling doubtful about Father's supposed drunken fall. The shard on the vanity and the strange circumstances made me question if Father's death was truly accidental, stirring a quiet suspicion in my mind. My gaze drifted, almost unconsciously, toward the doorway and to the stairs above, where the shard lay waiting on my vanity.

A drunken fall? No.

It was too simple, almost too obvious to be true. Father's recent agitation and William's warning at the ball had to have a connection somehow; the reality of it all began to press forward in a way I could not dismiss. If I could learn more, perhaps the unease within me would quiet, or at the very least allow me the truth I needed to grieve in peace.

I lifted my teacup, though my hands had begun to tremble. "I think," I said slowly, more to myself than to Mother, "there are still things I do not understand about that night."

And the grief that had held me so firmly began to shift, making room for something else entirely, an almost reckless determination to adhere to the final words Father spoke to me. "Seeing clearly is a gift," he had said, a gift that I possessed. I felt, all at once, that I could not turn from it now, not when so much remained clouded. I stood from my chair in the dining room and resolutely headed to grab the one clue that held the truth to my father's murder-the shard of glass.

Chapter Four:

Spirits

Mr. Moore had been Aunt Charlotte's head of staff for longer than I had been alive. His loyalty to duty made it easy to predict his whereabouts at any given moment. He most likely would be in the entry hall, preparing to see Aunt Charlotte off for any afternoon business she may have to attend to. I entered through the great doors and found him, sure enough, just within, his usual air of attentiveness and formality displayed on his face, as though nothing in the world, not even death itself, could ruffle the order he so carefully maintained. He inclined his head towards me, and his expression eased with quiet concern.

"Miss Bridget. I trust you rested, at least a little."

"As well as might be expected," I replied, feeling a hollow ache in my chest. "Mr. Moore, I hoped you might assist me with something."

He stepped aside at once, guiding me toward the small side table near the window, away from the bustle of the hall.

"Anything within my power, miss."

I drew the shard carefully from my sleeve and held it out to him. "This was found in the garden the night of my father's fall. I wondered if you recognized the bottle it came from."

Mr. Moore accepted it with both hands, turning it thoughtfully in the light. His brow furrowed almost at once. "No, miss," he said after a moment. "I do not believe this came from our stores."

"You're certain?" I said, astonished.

"Quite certain." He glanced up at me, his tone respectful but firm. "The glass appears to bear the crest of a lion. Hartwood does not keep such wine. It is, forgive me, of a very poor quality. Almost bitter, hardly suitable for a household of this standing." The confirmation sent a quiet ripple through me.

"Where might one purchase it?" I asked.

He hesitated only briefly. "Most likely the Stag and Crown, Miss. They keep a stock of cheaper bottles for travelers and the like. It is not an uncommon fare there."

The Stag and Crown. Even hearing the name stirred an old discomfort I had long tried to ignore. I had never liked the place. It stood on the road toward Ashcombe, always busy, always loud, its windows glowing late into the night. I had known years ago that the establishment was often frequented by my father, a peculiar choice for a man of his station. As I matured, I came to realize what this usually meant. Gambling. And while there had not been a whisper of this habit uttered to me by anyone, it always seemed to hover around in the air unacknowledged and uncomfortable. I had seen enough to know what his late returns and quiet arguments with Mother truly meant. I loved my Father, though, and had learned to push the thought of his mistakes from my mind whenever it surfaced. It was easier to remain ignorant than to accept that he was being reckless and possibly even risking our family's fortune. Yes, far easier to pretend that these things only happened to other men of less caliber, not my father. And yet, standing there with the shard of cheap wine in my hand, the memory of those long absences and unspoken tensions seemed to crowd my mind.

If the bottle had come from the Stag and Crown, then it had not been meant for Hartwood at all, raising the question of how it ended up there on the night my father died, and what secrets it might reveal about his activities.

I set off back to the cottage to grab my cloak and prepare for a discreet walk into town. The fewer people who knew of my investigation, the better. I kept my cloak drawn close, the shard tucked safely within my sleeve, and the weight of secrecy enveloped me.

The afternoon breeze was cool, prompting me to keep my cloak wrapped tightly around me. Eventually, I rounded a corner and spied my destination. The Stag and Crown, a lowly, almost pathetic building, held together with a low roof and wide front windows. I noticed the steady puff of smoke rising from the large chimney, and my nerves began to rise along with it. This place was the stage for a side of my Father that I had never wished to know about and tried to ignore, and yet, here I was, about to set foot in it. As I drew closer, voices, some booming and others solemn, drifted out from within. I shuddered slightly, took a deep breath, and crossed the threshold.

Mr. Mason stood behind the counter. He had owned The Stag and Crown for many years. His broad frame was hunched, and his expression fixed in its usual state of impatience. He looked up as I approached, surprise flickering briefly before settling into a wary frown.

"Evenin', miss," he muttered. "Not often we see ladies of your sort in here." No doubt he knew who my father was, but whether or not he knew I was Lord Hartwood's daughter remained a mystery to me. I decided it was best to keep it that way.

"I shan't keep you long," I said, placing the shard upon the counter between us. "I hoped you might recognize this bottle."

He picked it up, squinting at the bottle, and gave a short grunt.

"That one? Aye, we keep it. Cheap table red, Lion's Blood we call it. Comes in by the crate, sells quickly to travelers and men who don't much care what they're drinking."

"Do you recall who purchased it recently?" I inquired.

His mouth tightened as he seemed reluctant to answer. "Couldn't say. Had a whole case go missing last week, though. Stolen clean from the back. That's all I know of it."

"Stolen?" I repeated, unable to hide my astonishment.

He nodded once, already turning away as though the matter no longer concerned him. "Like I done said, that's all I know of it."

There was nothing else to gain from him. I thanked him and stepped back into the evening, the door closing behind me with a dull thud.

The walk back felt quieter, the sun sinking low and casting long, golden streaks across the fields. The air had cooled even more, and a faint smell of smoke drifted from distant chimneys. By the time Hartwood's grounds came into view, the lanterns were being lit one by one along the paths, their small flames flickering to life against the gathering dusk.

The groundskeeping men moved steadily between them, poles in hand, their silhouettes dark against the fading light. As I passed, one of them glanced up. It was Antonio.

He raised a hand in a small greeting as he smiled faintly. It was nothing, no more than a polite acknowledgement, but I felt heat rush to my face all the same.

"Miss Hartwood," he said, lowering the pole and stepping toward me, his expression shifting from concentration to something gentler. "You should not be out alone at this hour."

"I have only just come from the village," I replied. "The road is hardly dangerous."

"I do not doubt it," he said, his eyes seemed to linger on my face longer than they should have. "But I would sleep more easily knowing you arrived home safely. Might I accompany you the rest of the way?"

The remark was so casually spoken, I almost missed the warmth beneath it. "You may," I replied, a flutter of excitement passed over me as he fell into step beside me, his pace unhurried, careful to match mine.

"You work late," I said after a moment, watching him tug at his work gloves, the day's labor evident in their wear.

"There is always something that needs tending," he replied lightly. "Lanterns do not light themselves after all," he teased.

I smiled despite myself. "And you never tire of it?"

"Oh, I do," he said lightly. "But caring for beautiful things is something my father raised me always to do." His eyes met mine, and I couldn't help but wonder if he was referring not just to the estate, but to me.

"Well, you are very good at it," I said. "The gardens have never looked finer."

That earned me a small, crooked smile.

"So is your father on staff here as well?" I prodded, hoping to learn more about him.

"My father has been unwell," he said simply. "What I earn goes toward his care." There was no self-pity in his tone, only matter-of-fact devotion.

"That is a great responsibility," I said quietly.

"It is only what anyone would do."

Not anyone, I thought. But I did not say it aloud. "And your mother? How is she faring with his illness?"

"My mother passed away when I was very young. She herself was a great beauty, cared for immensely by my father. He would always say people were the greatest treasures in life, not to let little moments pass without savoring them, because before you know it, those treasures could be gone."

"I am so sorry for your loss." I couldn't help but feel a strong bond with him; it was as if we were both carrying the same weight of losing a parent, and that connection made me want to share even more with him.

"And you?" he asked, turning the conversation with gentle ease. "I know I am not the only one to experience great loss. How do you fare tonight?"

I hesitated. "Some moments are easier than others."

He smiled slightly at me, encouraging me to go on.

"It feels almost as if I am walking through a thick fog, and no matter what I do, it does not dissipate."

He nodded thoughtfully, as if it were a feeling he knew all too well. "Well, if it is any consolation, you certainly do not seem lost," he said. This observation caught me off guard. How much attention had he been paying me?

"And how is that, might I ask?" I questioned.

"I simply mean, it seems rather robust of you to be out and about. Most people would confine themselves to the solitude of their home upon the loss of a loved one for weeks, maybe months. But not you, here you are, out and about, making calls just a few days after. You are quite an impressive person," he stated with a cheeky smile. I felt a warmth rise to my cheeks as I looked away, embarrassed by how easily his words unsettled me in an exciting sort of way.

"You are very bold in your language, sir, and quite observant," I said.

"If one pays attention, people reveal who they are long before they speak it," he replied.

The cottage came into view ahead, its windows glowing softly.

"You need not walk me further," I said, though I found I did not quite wish for him to leave.

He slowed, but did not step away just yet. "I do not mind," he said. "It is pleasant company." He smiled just slightly. I could not help but return the smile. A small silence radiated between us, and I felt my spirits jolting with excitement.

He bowed politely, stepping back at last. "Do try to rest well, Miss Hartwood. I wish I could say the fog clears completely, but some pain we carry with us forever, I fear. You just need to find the right people who will accompany you through it."

"I shall try," I replied, "Thank you for your warmth and kindness. It has been most refreshing."

I turned toward the dimly lit path leading to the front door of the cottage. I could almost feel his eyes linger on me before hearing his footsteps take off. Something new and unfamiliar began to thread its way through my grief. Not relief, not peace, but an impalpable interest. I raised my hand to turn the knob of the front door, and felt the weight of the glass shard hidden in my sleeve press itself into my skin ever so slightly. The sudden reality of my present circumstances resurfaced. How silly was I? My father had scarcely passed away, our lives hung in the imbalance of uncertainty, and here I was, dazed by the attention of a mere stranger, as if I were a girl with nothing heavier on her mind than the next dance. How absurd. I could not help but feel ashamed and embarrassed.

Before I turned the doorknob completely, I recalled a thought I had had on my walk back from the Stag and Crown, that I ought to check the cellar's ledger. I turned and quickened my pace back towards the servant's entrance of Hartwood. There was more information to seek after, and I did not want to wait until tomorrow. The sun began its descent under the horizon, so I quickened my pace. I subconsciously peered around the grounds, hoping to see Antonino's figure in the distance, but he was nowhere to be seen. I shook my head, as if hoping to shake him from my mind. It did not feel appropriate to allow these emotions to stir within me when it seemed like my heart held no more room for anything other than mourning.

I entered the servant's hall and soon found Mrs. Weatherby, the housekeeper, directing one of the maids with a brisk authority. She turned at the sound of my steps, her brows lifting in mild surprise at finding me there.

"Miss Bridget," she said. "Is something amiss?"

"I beg your pardon for intruding," I replied, lowering my voice instinctively in the servant's quarters. "I wondered if I might see the cellar ledger from the night of the ball. Only for a moment."

I followed her to the small office across from the large kitchen, where all the ledgers were stored neatly. She kindly opened the book to the appropriate date.

"There you are," she said, stepping aside, "Mr. Moore insists on exactness with inventory, so you will find the information here to be accurate."

"Thank you, Mrs. Weatherby," I said as I leaned over the book, my eyes moving quickly over the careful script. Wine, champagne, port —each item noted, removed, and returned. And then I found what I had been looking for. One full bottle of brandy. Withdrawn by Lord James Richard Hartwood himself. No mark was noted to signify the bottle's return. I read the line over again as my pulse quickened. So the bottle was missing; it had never been brought back to the cellar.

"How very peculiar," I muttered under my breath.

Mrs. Weatherby gave me an inquisitive look, but I offered no explanation, and she was not one to pry. I thanked her and closed the ledger carefully, my thoughts jumping ahead. If Father had taken brandy into the garden that night, why had he been found beside a shattered bottle of that cheap– what did Mr. Mason call it again? Oh, right, "Lion's Blood" wine? Where had the brandy gone?

I was still turning this over as I stepped back into the servant's hall, preparing to make my way out, when a voice behind me called softly, "Pardon me, miss."

I turned to find one of the footmen standing a few paces away, hat in hand, his expression uncertain.

"Yes?"

"I thought it might be of use," he said carefully. "The night of your father's… accident. I was in the corridor near the back when I saw Mr. Finch pass through toward the garden. Not long after your father went out."

"Mr. Finch?" I repeated, rather alarmed.

He nodded. "Yes, miss. Lord James had what looked to be a bottle of brandy with him. I noticed it because he nearly dropped it on the steps. Then, some minutes later, Mr. Augustus Finch went the same way. Seemed in a hurry."

The words settled over me slowly, like dust. Augustus Finch. My father's closest friend, for as long as I could remember. A man who had dined at our table, walked our grounds, laughed beside him, countless evenings. Why would he be following Father into the garden that night? And why, if Father had carried brandy, had he been found beside wine? Where had the brandy bottle gone?

It has become very apparent that William knows more than he has let on. Perhaps his distance from me has nothing to do with his possible engagement to Miss Isabelle, but rather, more to do with his Father's sinister role in my father's death. The thought of it left me unsettled, but guided me nonetheless towards the next step. If there was truth to uncover, William would know it, or at least more than I.

I noticed the footman looking around, too awkward to leave without a reply from me. "Thank you," I interjected quickly, "yes, thank you, that is most helpful." He held the door open for me as I left. I was carrying a great deal of information to process. I had to assume that everything I had seen up until this point was true, but I found that difficult. I had to trust that Mr. Moore kept accurate records from that night, that this footman was being honest with me about seeing Mr. Finch in a location that would place Mr. Finch with my father mere moments before his death, that Mr. Mason, the barkeeper, really did have a case of the same wine stolen from the pub last week. Everyone seemed to have bits and pieces of information that seemed to lead me away from suspecting their own involvement in the matter. I felt a strong need to speak to my dear friend William about it; he had always been a confidant of mine, but it seemed as if he were somehow involved in the matter as well. I could use this to my advantage; it meant he would have more information, which I could retrieve from him. Perhaps he could help uncover answers to the many questions swirling through my mind.

Chapter Five:

Old Friends, Older Secrets

The Finch Family were dear friends of ours. Augustus had met my father, James, when they were both serving in the Army Commissions many years ago. My father was a young Lieutenant, and Augustus was in his regiment. They seldom spoke of what had happened during their few years serving, but that experience formed an unbreakable bond between the two. After their service, Augustus returned to build a banking business. Father aided him in this venture, introducing him into high society and gaining clients for him. Over time, "Finch Financial and Bank" became the only bank trusted implicitly by almost the entire county. The two men seemed to balance one another out in a way that led to great success. Father was impulsive and charismatic; Augustus was measured and composed. Augustus gained great wealth and purchased a small estate only a few hours' carriage ride from Ashcombe Park. Their proximity only meant our relationship with them grew stronger. Holidays, dinners, picnics, and countless small favors were exchanged between families without ceremony. Some of the happiest times of my life were in the company of my parents and the Finches. So it was not odd that the next morning, Mother informed me that Mrs. Eleanor Finch had invited us, in her friendly yet insistent manner, to join them for afternoon tea, "if only to provide a change of scenery and to enjoy the comfort of familiar company."

Mrs. Finch absolutely adored order and propriety. One never doubted that her household moved precisely as she wished. Her form was rather round, much like that of her husband's, and her manner was always gracious. They had two children, William, who had inherited her calm confidence, and Ruth, a bright and energetic girl with red hair and freckles across her face. She was not yet old enough to conceal her thoughts behind politeness, and, much to the dismay of her governess, was often found running amok. She was both mischievous and clever, traits I had often hoped would never be ironed out by age and expectations.

It was refreshing to return to their home, but it felt both natural and painful. It served as a reminder that this, too, was not the same without Father.

We were received in the drawing room, where the windows were open to admit the mild afternoon air. Conversation began as such things must—with condolences, soft inquiries after our health, and a careful avoidance of anything too sharp or immediate. But grief, I was learning, did not respect the boundaries of polite conversation. Halfway through the tea time, Mother's composure faltered. Her teacup rattled faintly against the saucer, and then she pressed a hand to her mouth as a sob escaped her. Mrs. Finch rose at once.

"Oh my poor dear," she said gently, though her tone left no room for hesitation. "Give us a moment, if you please, all of you."

While this request was directed towards her own family, I took my leave of the room as well, seeking an opportunity to speak with William more privately. The rest of the family had made their way out into the garden, and I was sure William would attempt to slip away for an afternoon ride on his horse. Luckily, I caught up to him before he could flee.

“Would you care for a turn about the garden?” I asked. His eyes did not meet mine, as if looking at me would cause him pain. “I won’t take too much of your time,” I implored.

“Yes, of course,” he managed. I wish he knew how much his coldness was adding to the hurt already bursting within me. We took off side by side into the gardens. They were far smaller than Charlotte’s, but still held beauty nonetheless. The paths were still damp from the cool of the morning.

We walked in silence at first, the gravel crunching softly beneath our steps. At last, I spoke.

“William… What do you know of my father’s death?”

He stopped short. The surprise was there, though brief, before he composed himself. But I had known him too long not to see it. The uneasy tug at his cuff, the way his gaze shifted, the effort it took to appear steady.

“You should not concern yourself with such things,” he said at last, his voice low. “It will not help you.” He began to tug once again at the cuff on his sleeve.

“I found a shard of bloodied glass in the gardens back at Hartwood,” I admitted. “It matches the bottle found near my father’s body. I believe it to be a clue that hints at something darker behind his death.”

He exhaled slowly, running a hand over the back of his neck.

“Bridget… please. I know it is hard, but you must leave it be. The authorities have deemed it an accident, and there are forces at play here that you do not understand. Looking into it further will only place you in danger."

There it was again. Danger. He was trying to protect me from something. "What forces?" I pressed. "Is it to do with your father? Something is amiss here, and I believe you know what it is."

He looked away then, out beyond the gardened land, surely wishing he were riding his horse rather than having this conversation. I could sense the conflict within him.

"I wish," he said quietly, in an effort to keep others from hearing, "that I could tell you my father is completely innocent. But these past few months," He hesitated, as though the admission itself cost him something. "He has shown me that his morals are not what I believed them to be, and as much as I want to admit to him my disapproval, these matters require delicacy and efficient timing."

The confession struck harder than I expected. He had always been so brave; I had never known him to care what others thought, including his parents, which made his silence on the matter all the more unnerving. Could I trust him? His broad shoulders were carrying much lately. I wished he would let me help him carry the load. I longed for him to confide in me, but one of his greatest strengths was now one of his greatest faults- his all-encompassing need to protect those he cared about. If he had made it up in his mind that it would protect not only me, but his family as well, to keep me in the dark, then he would take the truth to his grave. I won't be able to obtain any further information from him on this subject. A deep disappointment prevailed over me.

"And what of Miss Isabelle?" I interjected.

"Miss Isabelle? What of her?" He replied, surprised.

"Is the timing of all of this "efficient" enough for your engagement? Perhaps her fortunes can save you from whatever it is you're trying to hide."

He looked hurt, "Bridget, I…"

But before he could respond, a voice called out from the path behind us.

"William! Mama says we are to come in at once. Lady Hartwood is feeling better, but wishes to return home soon." Ruth stood there, hands clasped, her eyes moving between us with open curiosity. We stepped apart at once, the moment broke as cleanly as if it had never existed.

"Thank you, Ruth," William said as he turned and bowed in my direction, "Miss Hartwood." He then took his leave and headed for the stables. Dejected, I headed back inside to the drawing room to collect Mother. We bid our farewells and boarded our carriage back to the cottage. The late afternoon had become greyed by clouds, threatening, but unwilling, to rain. My thoughts were unclear, as if a picture were being painted in my mind, but it was nowhere near complete enough to make out what the painting was even of. Pieces of it I had collected up to this point were William's warning and doubt in his own father, the wine glass, the missing brandy, and Augustus following Father into the garden. I had so hoped that speaking with William would ease my mind, that some explanation might be offered to redirect my suspicions to somewhere else. But instead, it had done the opposite. My fears had been confirmed, and for the first time, the possibility that Augustus Finch, my father's oldest friend, had a hand in his death no longer felt like an untenable absurdity, but something far worse- something that in the end might prove to be true.

Chapter Six:

A Welcome Distraction

The afternoon grew late as I walked the gardens, hoping the air might settle the restless thoughts that had followed me from my conversation with William. Though we were not on good terms, it was almost as if the thought of him, the idea that there was ever a time when we could have been together, buoyed me, keeping me from drowning in this sea of uncertainty. I tried to pretend that Miss Isabelle did not exist, or that I was in her place, and she in mine instead. The paths I perused were neat as ever, the hedges trimmed, and every piece of gravel seemed to keep to its allotted place. Aunt Charlotte kept her grounds with a precision that bordered on devotion. I turned along the lower path near the fountain and saw a familiar figure some distance ahead, kneeling beside a flowerbed, sleeves rolled up slightly.

Antonio. I hesitated, suddenly uncertain if I should engage in conversation or turn back. He looked up at the sound of my steps and rose at once, setting his trowel down.

"Good afternoon, miss," he said, bowing his head politely.

"Good afternoon," I returned. "I hope I am not interrupting your work."

"Not at all. The roses will forgive me a moment's neglect."

I allowed myself a faint smile at that.

"The gardens are looking especially fine today," I said. "You and the others have done a remarkable job; no doubt my Aunt is pleased with your work."

"I hope it is not just your Aunt that feels pleased with my work," he posed, a test to see if I would play along with his interest. I felt my stomach twist in knots, my blushing cheeks revealing my true feelings without my consent.

"Cousin Rupert has never been a great outdoorsman, though I'm sure he enjoys the fruits of your labors from the windows," I replied.

He laughed, loud and unrestrained, "Have you always been such a tease, miss? It truly is a wonder no man has stolen your hand in marriage yet. Surely there have been many an offer you have declined?"

I smirked. I did not want to indulge him, but I also did not wish to reveal how there had been no offers of marriage. Up until recently, I believed, along with most other people, for that matter, that William would make me an offer, but no such offer had come, and now he was in the grasp of Miss Isabelle, and I felt destined for a long and lonely life.

He must have felt the shift in my mood as his expression softened. I felt him regard me with a quiet seriousness as he sat on his work stool.

"How are you, really?" he asked gently. His sincerity caught me off guard and pulled at my heart in a somewhat delightful way.

“I must confess,” I said, voice trembling slightly, “my life does not feel like my own. Everything has changed, and I cannot seem to come to terms with it.”

He nodded as though he understood.

“I am sorry how the wine affected him so poorly that night,” Antonio said softly, his eyes lowering to the gravel at his feet. “Some men never know when it has turned against them.”

I gave a small nod, the memory pressing in with sudden weight. “As you know, I know a thing or two about losing a parent,” he stated, “I know that kind of loss, it is not something you can simply pick yourself up from quickly.”

“Yes,” I said quietly. “What helped you? Pick yourself up after your mother…” I trailed off, not even wanting to utter the words.

“Well,” he began, “I know this is probably not what you want to hear, but I will say it gets better with time.”

“Ah… time,” I muttered, “It goes by so painfully slow right now, I do not know how I can wait for time to heal the damage that has been done.”

He regarded me with a sincerity I had often felt from William, so it felt slightly misplaced for him to be looking at me similarly. A few moments of silence passed, then he slapped his hands to his knees and stated, “I can think of something that might help the time go by faster for you, m’lady.” he had a mischievous gleam in his eye. My guard suddenly went up, but I couldn’t help but smile at his playfulness.

“And what is that, sir?” I responded, curiosity brimming. How had he taken such a solemn moment and turned it into something almost… good?

"Close your eyes," he suggested. I gave him an unapproving and confused glance. "Trust me," he continued. So I did. I closed my eyes and listened as I heard him rise from his seat and make his way over to me. He was so close I nearly felt his breath on my face. What was happening? Was he about to break all sense of propriety and kiss me? I was not sure how I felt about it, but I wasn't stopping him either. Then all of a sudden, I felt something cold and squishy smudge all over my nose and cheek. I immediately opened my eyes to learn he had smeared mud all over my face. I could not believe it! I stood facing him, my mouth agape with shock; his eyebrows were raised, and a deep smile emboldened his countenance.

"Why, I have never," I protested, when all of a sudden another clump of mud landed directly on the shoulder of my dress.

"Ha, ha!" He laughed, "Come now, Miss Hartwood, allow yourself a moment's freedom."

I paused, then decidedly bent down to pick up clumps of mud myself and threw them as hard as I could in his direction. One landed directly on his chest, the other on his leg.

"That's it, miss!" he yelled as we laughed and tossed more and more clumps back and forth.

Suddenly, we heard a carriage approaching, and the fear of being discovered in such a state proved stronger than the enjoyment of the moment.

"Quick! Follow me this way," he said, as he ran swiftly towards a large grove of trees bordering the estate in the direction of the cottage. I followed suit, certain he was heading for the small pond that lay just beyond the cottage.

We arrived at the pond not long after, quietly giggling like children, hoping that our escapade had no witnesses. He began to clean the mud from his work gloves, and I hurriedly tried to clean it from my own hands and dress as best I could. There would be no good explanation to Mother about this. Hopefully, only Jane would see me like this; surely she would help keep this a secret.

Some minutes passed, and Antonio seemed to have regained as much cleanliness as he could.

"Well, I must thank you for the distraction; it has been most invigorating," I stated.

"Do not thank me," he said, his voice suddenly lower than before, "distraction or not, I know the minute you walk back to the cottage, the grief will most likely take its hold once again," he said sadly, "but I am glad to have seen your smile."

I smiled back at him, suddenly taking in the beautiful scene surrounding us. A serene, deep-blue pond, bright green moss growing on the surrounding rocks and trees, and there was a crispness in the air. I did not wish for the moment to end. I did not wish for the grief to come back, but I already began to feel it creeping its way into my heart.

"I am so sorry, I have upset you," he came and sat near me, "that was not my intention, please forgive me."

"No, no, you have gifted me a moment's leisure, a true reprieve from all this heaviness and uncertainty." I did not want him to feel guilty for the welcome distraction he had so willingly given me. His eyes were so kind, and he seemed perfectly at ease.

He did not press further, only waited, attentive and patient, and something in his manner—so steady, so removed from the politics and expectations of any families involved—made it easier to speak freely with him. I so desperately wanted to confide in someone, tell someone about my little discoveries, and Antonio granted me the space to do so.

"I cannot help feeling there is more to it," I admitted. "More than a fall. I have tried to leave it alone, but I cannot."

His gaze sharpened, his tone a little surprised. "What have you found, miss?"

"Very little," I said. "Only fragments. But enough to spark my curiosity."

I told him of the shard and about how strange it was to find wine instead of brandy near his person. I told him of how the more time passed, the more uneasy I felt about his death. He listened respectfully and attentively, his eyes fixated on a squirrel climbing a tree across the pond.

"Do you suspect anyone of foul play?" he asked at last.

I hesitated a moment, then admitted, "Mr. Augustus Finch." I hated admitting that; it felt like a huge betrayal of a man who had appeared to be nothing but good his whole life. But appearances can be deceiving.

Antonio's reaction was swift, though subtle—an alertness in his posture, a clenching of his jaw.

"Augustus Finch? Is this that large fellow with the great moustache?"

"Yes, it is," I responded.

"I saw him that night, come to think of it," Antonio said slowly and carefully, as though he was recalling something from a random part of his memory. "I was lighting the lanterns along the paths when I noticed him leaving the garden. He seemed unsettled. In a hurry, as though he did not wish to be seen."

The words struck me harder than I expected.

"You are certain?" I asked.

"Quite certain, if we're thinking of the same man, that is. I've only seen him a couple of times in passing, but it did seem to be him, or someone resembling him."

My thoughts spun at once. Augustus had followed Father into the garden. The brandy was missing. The wine did not belong to Hartwood. It began to take shape in an eerie way.

"But how?" I murmured. "How could he have done it, and why? What was his motive to murder his closest friend in the whole world?"

"Some people make hasty decisions; perhaps it was simply just an accident?" Antonio suggested, he watched me with a steady, searching look, his deep green eyes made me feel both seen and excitedly nervous all at once.

I drew a breath, aware suddenly of the time.

"I must return," I said. "Dinner with Aunt Charlotte, I mustn't be late, and I will take ages to prepare myself sufficiently," I said, gesturing to my muddied apparel.

He nodded as he attempted to hold back a laugh at my tousled appearance. As I turned to go, his hand caught mine, and I felt frozen in place. He placed a warm, gentle kiss on the top of my hand. As he let me go, he suggested, "I hope you will grant me the pleasure of your company soon, Miss Hartwood."

I managed a half smile, "Until next time," I promised as I quickly turned away, hoping to hide the annoying color that always seemed to rise to my face when I was around him. I was being so absurd, so naive to allow such feelings to ripple through me when everything else around me had changed so gravely. And yet, despite my embarrassment, his kindness threaded itself quietly through my thoughts as persistently as any question of wine or missing brandy. I told myself it meant nothing, but I could not quite convince my heart of that.

Chapter Seven:

Lord Rupert Hartwood

My soggy entrance into the cottage was met by Mr. Smith, who was far better than Mother seeing me in such a state, but not as good as Jane finding me. I could not rely upon him not to tell Mother of what he saw. I could only hope he'd spare her the stress. I uttered a sincere apology for the drips as I hastened up the stairs to wash up for dinner as best I could. Mother must have been preoccupied with getting ready herself, and Jane nearly ran into the wall when she entered my room and found me frantically attempting to wash any sign of dirt from my hair in the basin.

"Please, Jane, I need your help. If Mother sees me like this, I will never hear the end of it," I pleaded.

"Of course, m'lady, straight away!" She rolled up her sleeves and set to work, scrubbing and combing through the mangled mess of my hair. I knew I could rely on her efficiency and discretion, and was so relieved for her assistance.

Over an hour passed, and we finally exited my bedroom to find Mother waiting in the front room by the fire.

"Well, that took much longer than expected. I hope we have not kept Charlotte and Rupert waiting too long; it is expedient for us to remain in their good graces," she pointed out.

We made the short walk up to the Estate, and Aunt Charlotte met us just within the entry hall. She looked radiant as always. Beautiful jewels adorned her neck, the perfect accent to her maroon silk dress. She had a light about her, and it felt almost like the room brightened in response to her presence. Her voice was warm, and if she felt upset about our slight tardiness, she showed no sign of it.

"My dears," she said, taking Mother's hands in hers. "You look quite worn. We shall remedy that with a proper meal and company. Come, Rupert is in the drawing room."

Rupert stood near the hearth, exactly where I expected to find him. Tall, angular, and perpetually uncomfortable in his own limbs, he inclined his head when we entered, his greeting quiet and slightly delayed, as though each word had to be considered before it left him.

"Lady Rosamund, Miss Bridget."

He said little more after that, retreating into his usual stillness. To most, Rupert might have seemed cold or aloof, but I had never thought so. There was an honesty about him, a complete lack of pretense. He did not flatter, did not charm, did not perform the small social theatrics expected of gentlemen. He simply was as he appeared— a bit awkward, deep in thought, and entirely uninterested in impressing anyone. Charlotte had tried for many years to find a suitable match for him, but his total lack of interest in it always made any arrangement fail miserably. As much as she wanted him to marry and have the halls at Hartwood be filled with her grandchildren's laughter, she never wanted to force him into a life he did not want to live, a rare quality among nobility. She came to accept his solitary preferences. I had always found his presence refreshing.

Charlotte, with her effortless charity and poise, filled the room with conversation, stories, and gentle humor; her presence seemed to soften the room's tension, almost as if she alone were keeping grief at bay by refusing to let silence enter.

"But enough of my babbling, how are you getting on, truly, Rosamund?" she entreated.

"Quite well, thanks to your great generosity, I do not know where we would be without you," Mother responded.

"Pish posh, we do what we can for family, isn't that right, Rupert?" Charlotte suggested. Rupert only nodded his head as he continued reading from his newspaper.

"How is the cottage? I have plans to replace the linens with some lovely lavender ones I found while in London last season," Charlotte said.

The conversation carried on in much the same way until a footman entered and informed us that dinner was ready, so we all moved into the neat and perfectly arranged dining room. Mother and Charlotte's conversation continued to drivel on, and I had a hard time focusing. I attempted the occasional laugh when they laughed, but the sound of it felt hollow even to myself. It seemed as if their conversation required an enthusiasm I simply could not summon. I attempted to look interested, but my thoughts were elsewhere. Torn between my conversation with William, the afternoon with Antonio, and the same unanswered questions surrounding Father's death.

And then, right as the serving plate found its way to Rupert, it struck me quite suddenly.

Rupert! That's right, Rupert! The night of the ball, I had seen him running towards the entryway, most likely the first to reach the body before the alarm spread through the house. How had I not thought to ask him sooner? The realization settled over me, bringing with it a flicker of urgency.

I glanced across the table at him. He ate quietly, as he always did, his gaze lowered, his movements measured and deliberate. He had said little since we sat down, offering only the occasional response when Charlotte addressed him directly. I had to ask him about it. Of course, this was hardly the place to question him. Not here, beneath Charlotte's attentive gaze and Mother's fragile composure, with servants moving quietly in and out and every word weighed by civility. No, there would be a better moment.

After dinner, we moved, as Charlotte preferred, to the library for drinks and conversation. The large fireplace lit the room with a soft warmth, making it feel immensely welcoming. Books lined the walls, and I could not help but wonder if Rupert had read most, if not all of them. Charlotte joined Mother by the fire as they continued their light conversation. I spied Rupert sitting in his usual spot in a rather large chair near the window. He loved to be half-removed from the center of conversation, to be near what was going on, but not to be a part of it. There was no pretense about him—no effort to charm or impress. He spoke when he had something worth saying and remained silent when he did not.

"Cousin," I said softly.

He turned, surprised, then inclined his head, looking up at me from above the silver rims of his spectacles, "Miss Bridget."

"I hoped I might speak with you about the other night."

He hesitated, then nodded and shifted slightly closer to the window, away from Charlotte and Mother's conversation. I sat in the chair across from him.

"I suspected you might inquire about this sooner or later," he commenced, "you have always been a very astute girl. Why, I recall a time when you were very young, five perhaps, you and your Mother had joined us for afternoon tea."

I bit my lip, attempting to hold back the desire to push the conversation past his story. While he was a quiet man, one-on-one conversations encouraged him to offer lengthy commentary.

"You were quite out of sorts and kept bringing up that the water in the front pond was strange, but she had not noticed anything of the sort," he continued. "Your mother gently quelled your little complaints there, but you kept asking why the insects were gone, why the algae had been cleared, no ducks were swimming on its surface... until finally you were asked to entertain yourself quietly with the nearby atlas. I had not thought much about this until the next day, when I learned that a stable boy clearing the troughs had misdirected the irrigation channel, causing the pond to change significantly. I was astonished at your ability to notice what was absent, while most only see what is present."

"That is very kind of you to remember," I stated, hoping to disguise my impatience, "I have always had a fondness for the grounds here at Hartwood." I glanced out the window at the nighttime scene. The lanterns were lit, and their glow lit the grounds like twinkling stars. The moon shone brightly over the large pond.

"A beautiful scene, is it not?" he implored, "Why, it was right here from this exact chair that I observed something most peculiar on the night you inquire of."

I leaned in closer, anxious for more information, nervous at what it might be.

"I left the frivolity of the party and decided to continue a reading I had started that morning on a recent study of amphibians, frogs, actually. The author suggests that their habits reveal much about the nearby land. I was most intrigued by their winter hibernation. Did you know some can survive nearly frozen? Extraordinary creatures. Entirely overlooked," he glanced toward the small table, as though he could still see the book resting there.

I cleared my throat to hopefully pull him out of pondering the significance of frogs.

He continued, "I had glanced up only for a moment as I turned a page, when I noticed your father walking from the garden towards the front of the house."

I felt my grip on the chair arm stiffen.

"He approached the steps unsteadily. I looked down at my book again for a mere moment, when something, there's no telling what, compelled me to look back out the window once more." His brow furrowed, the memory clearly fixed in his mind. "And he was there," Rupert said quietly, a lump seeming to have entered his throat. "Lying at the bottom of the stairs. Completely still."

My breath caught. "That quickly?" I asked.

He nodded. "It could not have been more than a couple of seconds," he said. "Not nearly enough time for him to have climbed even a few of the steps. And certainly not enough for a fall from the top."

The significance of this revelation confirmed my suspicions even more.

"If he had only climbed a couple of stairs," I uttered slowly, "then it is certain that the fall alone could not have killed him."

"Exactly!" Rupert agreed, his eyes aglow with a sort of frenzied concern, as if it were a matter he had been considering these past few days, greatly. "Even drunk, a man does not die from falling down a stair or two."

A chill crept through me—finally, someone else who had been wondering the same things I had.

"Then what happened?" I asked, my voice lower now. "What do you suppose was his undoing?"

Rupert hesitated, his fingers tapping once against the arm of the chair.

"I cannot say for certain," he admitted. "But I have read about substances, poisons, that do not act at once. They weaken the body, disrupt the senses. A man might feel faint or disoriented and appear drunk. He might lose his footing, but the toxins do not take their full effect for several minutes."

He glanced toward the shelves behind him.

"There is a volume," he added, almost absently. "On chemical agents. I read it last winter. It described certain compounds that leave no immediate sign. The victim grows weak, confused, and then collapses. To an observer, it might look no different than intoxication."

My mind seemed to be circling one single word: poison. That would explain why Father's brandy had gone missing, and why he had been drinking a cheap wine instead. But it still does not explain how this change occurred, or why.

"If that were true," I said slowly, "then the fall was only… the end of it, not the reason."

Rupert gave a small nod. "A possibility."

I could scarcely think past it. If there had been poison in the wine, if Father had been weakened before ever reaching the stairs, then his death might prove to be not so accidental after all.

"Rupert, what if I told you I still have a piece of the wine bottle from that night? Is there any way to test it and see if there is any trace of poison on it?"

He contemplated for a while and came up with, "Well, I suppose you could always do a rodent trial. Place the shard in a bowl of water, and place that bowl in a box with a captured rodent. If the rodent dies soon after, we could assume that the shard you found contains poison. If you bring it to me, I can conduct the experiment," he concluded, quite proud of his intellect.

"I will fetch the shard tomorrow and come deliver it directly to you in the morning before the service. The fewer people who know of this, the better," I declared.

We had our plan. I felt one large step closer to discovering the truth. Not long after our conversation, Mother inclined, "Come now, Bridget, we must be off. Tomorrow will be a long day with the funeral; we had better try to get some rest."

As Mother and I stepped back inside the small cottage later that night, Jane appeared at once from the hall.

"Oh, madam! You've returned. Mrs. Finch called for you and her daughter, Miss Ruth. They brought over a lovely bouquet this evening. It's in the front room—"

"Yes, thank you, Jane," I said, perhaps too quickly. "That was kind of her." I did not slow, moving past her and toward the stairs.

"Miss?" Jane called gently behind me.

"I only need a moment," I said, already halfway up. "Please don't trouble yourself."

At first glance, my room appeared just as I had left it– neat, orderly, a book upon my bed. But the shard— It was gone. I froze, my eyes scanning the surface of the vanity again, then the floor, the bedside table, and I searched all the drawers. My things had been moved, only slightly, but enough that I knew at once something was wrong. My comb was placed at a different angle. A book shifted. The chair was not quite where I had left it.

"Jane?" I called down to her from the top of the stairs, "Could you come here, please?" She appeared with a quickness to her step. "Jane, do you know what happened to that shard of glass that was lying atop my vanity?"

"No, miss. I haven't the foggiest." I eyed her most carefully; she seemed a bit dishevelled- her hair was slightly awry, her apron turned slightly to the left. A sign of her added responsibilities, possibly taking its toll on her. "So, you didn't take it and throw it out?"

"No, m'lady. The last I remember, you left the shard on top of the vanity. I have not touched it since." She explained.

Someone unwelcome had been in my room. Someone had taken it.

"Thank you, Jane, you may go."

I began to pace around my room, feeling a sudden burst of paranoia. It felt so alarming to think of someone rifling through my belongings without my permission. I tried to think of everyone who might have had access to my room since I last saw the shard here this morning. Jane, of course, Mr. Smith, and Mother would have had the easiest means to search my room. Then a sudden thought dawned on me.

"Wait a minute, Jane. Did Mrs. Finch deliver the flowers herself, or did she send someone else to deliver them?" I inquired, my voice shaky.

"It's like I said, miss. Mrs. Finch and her young daughter came by this evening to return your mother's shawl, which she had left behind from the afternoon tea at their home. They were so kind as to bring a lovely bouquet as well. They were saddened to have missed you and your mother. I invited them in for tea and a rest from the carriage ride. They stayed in the front room while I made up a tray for them in the kitchen... Oh, miss! You don't think..." her voice trailed off in shock and confusion.

"That they took the shard of glass?" I posed, "Yes, yes, I do."

Chapter Eight:

A Closed Door

A dreary gray filled the clouded sky with what felt like weather meant for mourning. The day itself seemed to know what lay in store: my father's funeral. I peered through the cottage window to find a light, misty fog settling over the pond and surrounding land, and felt a small chill run through me.

I got ready for the day slowly and quietly. Jane was uncharacteristically quiet as she hastened through her morning's duties. The fireplace had been tended to, a tray of food brought up to my room, and she was almost feverishly fitting me into my black gown. I was grateful for her quiet this morning. I finally sat where she positioned me, and was barely aware of her fixing my hair as my thoughts drifted towards the same uneasy conclusion: William had known. I had told him just yesterday about the shard, foolishly sharing my suspicions without gaining any further information. Of course, he would have told his father about my discovery. Augustus would have realized what it meant, that it somehow could be used as evidence of Father being poisoned. A cold certainty rose within me. Augustus had sent his wife and even his daughter to take the evidence from my room before I could act.

The thought made my stomach twist—not only with suspicion, but with something far sharper, betrayal. I had trusted

William. Trusted that whatever his father might be, he would stand apart from it. But perhaps I had been naïve. Blood and loyalty ran deeper than affection, deeper than truth.

Jane gently rested her hands on either of my shoulders, kindly, then left the room to tend to Mother. I stared at myself in the mirror for some time, then opened the vanity drawer to find my box of letters. I paused for a moment, contemplating whether reading a letter would pain me or not, and I decided to read one anyway. I pulled one from the bottom of the stack, hoping to find the comfort of an old friend. I opened it to find a letter William had sent me several years back, when I had been confined to my room with the fever. I had felt so miserable; little brought me comfort, though I remember his words encouraging me. The letter read:

Dear Bridget,

I do wish you would get well soon. It pains me to know you are stuck inside that dreadful room of yours with absolutely nothing to do but stare at the ceiling. Dinners without you and your family have become very dull. We are forced to listen to Father read every night now, and I find my mind is not meant for such intellectual matters. I would much rather be out riding or skipping rocks on the lake with you.

Mama says I must be patient, but I do not think patience is very useful when one's friend is confined to their bed. You had better recover promptly, or I shall be forced to come yell very bad jokes through your window until you laugh yourself well again.

Your friend,

William

I stared longingly at his name scrawled at the bottom of the page, and wished he had been capable of offering some measure of comfort to me in my time of need today as well.

"The carriage is ready for you, miss," Jane said softly, her words felt distant as I rose from my chair, feeling unprepared to face my father's funeral, yet knowing I must go.

Mother sat across from me, her eyes reddened from another restless night; no doubt. I could not tell whether she truly noticed anything, for she remained silent the entire ride. Whatever truths remained hidden from my view, whatever suspicions attempted to come to the forefront of my mind, they would have to wait. Today was for bidding my father farewell.

Aunt Charlotte, as always, had arranged everything. Nothing had been left unattended. She had ensured the day would be one of quiet dignity. Any last-minute confusions were unbeknownst to us, and I knew it was all thanks to her.

Upon entering the small church, I noticed several villagers from Ashcombe had gathered in the wooden pews. Some I had not known, others were familiar faces from my childhood- shopkeepers, tenants, familiar figures whose lives had long intersected with ours in small, ordinary ways. It did not take long for me to notice how very sparse the crowd was. Few nobility had come, no distant relations, no grand acquaintances from over the years; many of the pews in the small chapel remained vacant. It seemed Father had failed to make and keep many friends, which added to the unease of an already emotionally difficult day.

And then I saw them, the Finches. They stood near the front of the church, watching us solemnly as we took our own seats. Augustus and Eleanor were holding hands, as she dabbed at her eyes with her kerchief. Ruth stood on Mrs. Finch's other side, her demeanor pale and watchful. And there stood William, at the end of the pew opposite the aisle, furthest from me. His expression appeared unreadable as he kept his eyes fixed on the windows of the small church. They had come. The audacity of it—the calm, the composure, the quiet assumption of belonging—sent a sudden flare of anger through me so sharp it nearly eclipsed my grief. Augustus had followed Father into the garden that night. Most likely being the last person to speak with him before he died. The entire family seemed to have a part to play. Even little Ruth, with her cleverness, would have found it all too easy to retrieve a shard of glass from my room once asked to do so by her parents.

I could not help but keep my eyes from all of them; they stood dressed in black, as though they had every right to share in the sorrow of the day. The injustice of it rose within me, hot and immediate. How dare they come here to witness the burial of the man whose death they had all now had a hand in? I attempted with all my might to push them from my mind.

The service was short and seemed to end all too soon, just like Father's life. I remained beside the mound of fresh earth as people drifted past in hushed clusters, their condolences murmured as they made their way back toward the lane. I felt like I had hardly noticed them. I only felt the dampness of the day and how the air seemed to cling to everything– the grass, the headstone, the hem of my gown. The carved letters of Father's name upon the stone were still too new, too sharp, as though the smooth rock itself had not yet settled into the truth of it.

I feared greatly what his death meant for Mother and me, and though Charlotte was insistent on caring for us, I felt an immense pressure to marry someone who could help us out of our destitution. A memory of Father rose into my mind. I was a small girl, and we had gone out to the stables. He had lifted me onto a horse and was gently guiding the reins as we walked slowly. I remember shaking slightly from the nerves.

"Keep your head up, Bridget," he had cautioned. "Horses know when you are afraid, and it makes them afraid. Do not let the fear keep you from succeeding in this."

I recalled the warmth of his hand on mine, steadying me and drawing me from my fear. It had seemed such an ordinary moment that now felt impossibly distant, as if it were from another lifetime. Fear of what would come seemed to be filling the void he had left behind. I also felt a strong uncertainty about whether I had truly known who my father was. It seemed as though he had left more unsaid than understood now that he was gone. What did he do to give someone reason enough to murder him? I wiped at my eyes, but the tears continued to fall.

"Bridget." Someone gently called from behind.

I knew the voice before I turned.

William stood a few steps away, his expression drawn, his usual composure strained thin. He hesitated, as though unsure whether he had the right to approach, then closed the distance between us.

"I do not wish to intrude," he said softly. "But I could not leave without speaking to you."

I said nothing, turning back towards the grave.

I felt his apprehension, as if the cool breeze blew it my way.

"Bridget, I cannot bear to see you like this." His voice was low. I looked at him then, really looked, and saw how earnest he seemed, how restless. There was something unresolved in his expression—something he was holding tightly beneath the surface.

"You must know how much I care for you," he said, more urgently now. "Every day I have stayed away, every bit of distance that has formed between us, it has not been because of indifference. Keeping away from you has proven itself to be one of the hardest things I have ever done." He pulled at the cuff of his sleeve nervously, and I got the sense he wished to reach out for my hand, but something held him back from doing so.

"I have wanted to come to you, to offer any means of comfort, but I feared that doing so would only draw you further into something you do not understand." He hesitated and searched my face for any sign of forgiveness. I gave no such inclination.

"Then help me understand," I implored.

"I..." he paused for longer than expected, contemplating whether he would tell me the truth or not. He finally spoke, "I cannot.

I wish things were different, but it is too dangerous for you. I cannot…"

"Dangerous how?" I interrupted a bit more forcefully than I intended.

He sighed as he contemplated yet again whether or not to answer my question.

"I cannot explain," he said at last. "Not now. Perhaps not ever, please trust me in this."

A bitterness rose in my throat. His countenance had fallen.

"I cannot put my trust in you," I said. The words felt final, and I knew they would cause him pain; nevertheless, I continued. "Not now. Not after everything. You left me to wonder, to doubt, to whom could I confide? I have found more support and comfort from my maid and one of Charlotte's groundskeepers than I have from you. You pulled away when I needed you most, William. And now, you expect me to carry on happily without you, to feel sorry for you, and to somehow forgive you for withholding the truth from me."

Pain flickered across his face.

"I did it to protect you. I have been stepping in front of trouble for you since we were children, Bridget. I do not know how to stop, not now when the danger is much more serious."

"From what are you protecting me?" I demanded. "I deserve to know what I am up against."

He did not answer, only stared at me with his big brown eyes, the silence creating a great divide between us.

He stepped back, "I am sorry," he said quietly, "for everything."

Then, he turned and left, his pace quickening as though he feared he might falter in his composure if he lingered. It felt like the door that had been closing slowly for months now had finally shut and locked.

I watched him go, my chest aching with hurt, anger, and loss. When he disappeared beyond the path, I turned back to the headstone, my tears masked by the onset of light rain.

If William would not speak, if he would not give me the truth, then I would have to find it elsewhere. There was only one person left to speak to.

Mr. Augustus Finch.

Chapter Nine:

The Betrayal of a Letter

A few days passed in a slow blur, and it felt like everything had finally caught up to me. The finality of my conversation with William, the surety I felt that his father was responsible for my father's death, every bit of information I had collected in the past week had all placed a weight on top of me that made it now feel incredibly arduous even to leave my room. Mother was in a similar state and, at night, would come into my room and ask if we could sleep in the same bed because she could hardly be alone in hers. I had often contemplated confiding in her, but felt the burden would possibly break her beyond any possibility of repair, so I let her be.

I had been avoiding my next step of speaking with Mr. Finch. I didn't know where to start a conversation with him on this. There was a haunting fear that he might be someone entirely different from the man I knew growing up. He could be dangerous, even.

I spent the morning sitting by the window in my room, holding the box of letters from William, contemplating whether or not to toss them into the fire, when my eye caught hold of movement on the estate grounds. Though the cottage was somewhat secluded amidst a grove of trees, my window still overlooked the front of the Hartwood Estate, and pockets of it could be seen if one truly focused. I solemnly stared out my window and noticed the figures of several staff trimming the front lawn. I searched until my sight fixed on whom I believed to be Antonio. His broad shoulders and darker hair set him apart from the others, and I was glad for the distraction. My eyes began to close as I drifted off into a peaceful nap, when Mother's voice cut through the silence as she awoke from my bed.

"We must schedule a meeting with Augustus," she said. My eyes snapped open in a sudden shock at hearing his name spoken out loud. I looked at her, concerned that I had told her everything, that she did not believe me, and that she wanted to speak with him to prove me wrong.

"Yes, it is time. We must seek his counsel, see what is left for us, and finally face whatever remains. Augustus will know what is best for us," she declared.

The thought of asking for help from the man I most despised went against my very nature, but seeing as he was our financier and the most respected banker in the county, it would be foolish of us not to seek his counsel. Though skeptical that I was ready to meet with him, it did grant an opportunity that I might not feel brave enough to embrace in the future.

"You are right, Mother. It is time to do something more than wallow in our rooms," I agreed.

"Right then, I shall have Mr. Smith arrange a meeting for us to meet with him as soon as possible," she said as she wrapped her shawl around her and left the room. Relief mingled with a sharp twist of anxiety filled my frame.

I would be sitting across from Augustus in his office, speaking of how he could help us, when he was the one who had most likely put us in this predicament in the first place. Was it safe to even meet with him? I still have no clue why he would have wanted to end Father's life. Perhaps Antonio was right, perhaps it was just an accident, and Mr. Finch had simply been in the wrong place at the wrong time. But then, why go to such lengths to take the glass shard out of my possession, to dispose of something that could prove his guilt? And even William himself said that his father was not the man he thought he was, and that the situation was *dangerous*. Oh, William, the thought of him now allowed a bitter longing to permeate my being, and I wondered if I was making the right decision in following this suspicion.

The day passed, and Mr. Smith brought news that we could meet with Mr. Finch at his office the next day. I shivered at imagining myself in his office. Make no mistake, I would be watching—measuring every word, every look—trying to decide whether the man before me was still the one I had known, or if he was someone else entirely. Anxiety gnawed at my nerves, and I paced around my room for most of the night until Mother grew weary of the sound of my footsteps and insisted I get some rest, though my mind continued in a whirlwind of doubt and anticipation.

We awoke to a crisp, cool morning and spent the time getting ready for the outing. It took Jane longer to help us get ready, since we had completely neglected ourselves over the past few days. The carriage arrived for us after breakfast, and we made our way to Ashcombe. Finch Financial & Bank stood just off the main thoroughfare between the bookseller "Hobbs and Sons" and "The Light Post", a very popular inn. It was a bustling area because of the mail route that passed through, which made the quiet of the banking office all the more stark once we entered. Everything was orderly to the point of severity. Dark wood paneling lined the walls, and shelves were filled with ledgers and account books. The air smelled faintly of ink and leather.

Augustus rose at once when we entered, his expression carefully composed.

"Lady Rosamund," he said, bowing slightly. "Miss Bridget. I am glad you came." He gestured us to sit, his hands folded atop the desk, his expression composed. "I will speak plainly, Lady Rosamund," he said. "It is the only service I can offer you now."

Mother inclined her head stiffly. "Plainness is preferable. I understand the bleakness of our circumstances."

"Here it shows that the estate is entailed to a Henry Crawford — obviously, you know it cannot pass to Bridget," he continued. "That alone removes the house and lands from your control."

I felt Mother's hand tighten in her lap.

"And James' debts?" she asked.

Augustus glanced at me, then back to Mother. "They must be settled before anything else is considered. Creditors will have a first claim on the remaining assets—furnishings, investments, accounts, and any liquid funds. Gambling debts are particularly unforgiving, and your father's debts were quite extensive, to say the least. From what I can tell in his accounts, there is not enough money to keep the estate.

"Upon James' death, I wrote to Mr. Crawford and inquired if he would want to purchase the estate along with its debts, since he is the one who stands to inherit it, and he declined rather resoundingly. He said Lord James had ruined what was left of the Hartwood

Inheritance, and he would not inherit the debts James had so absurdly acquired."

Mother closed her eyes briefly. "What does that mean for us, then, Augustus?" she asked, her voice steady despite the seriousness of the matter.

"Let me see here," Augustus said as he sifted through a large bundle of papers, "it seems that you will retain your jointure from the marriage settlement. My records indicate it would be a very modest fixed income, but it would be enough to keep you afloat. The good news is that all your personal effects, such as jewelry and clothing, will remain yours. But beyond that," he hesitated, "you may need to continue to live quietly for an extended period of time. Take advantage of Charlotte's generosity as long as you can, or live on a smaller holding."

"And Bridget?" Mother pressed.

Augustus's gaze shifted to me again, measured, calculating in a way I could not quite read.

"Miss Hartwood's future will depend largely upon alliance," he said carefully. "A suitable marriage would secure her position, and yours. Without it, society is not kind to women left without fortune."

The conversation between him and Mother continued, but my growing anxiety was pulling my attention. My pulse beat loudly in my ears and seemed to drown out almost every word. I was acutely aware of the desk before us—the neat stacks of papers, the locked drawers, the sense that this room held more truth than Augustus was offering aloud.

Words, I realized suddenly, would not help me with my endeavors here. I could not ask him outright. I could not accuse him. If there were answers to be found, they would most likely be hidden.

"Forgive me," I said abruptly, my voice sounding steadier than I felt. "I find myself quite parched. Would it be possible to have some tea?"

Augustus turned toward me at once. "Of course, my child. Allow me."

He rang the bell, and when no one came, he excused himself to see that it was fetched, leaving the door closing softly behind him.

The moment it shut completely, I was on my feet.

Mother's eyes widened in alarm. "Bridget, whatever are you doing?"

"There is no time to explain," I whispered.

I moved quickly to the other side of the desk, my eyes jumping back and forth from the many papers atop it to the door. My heart was pounding so loud I was certain it could be heard from the corridor. I did not know exactly what I was looking for, but everything seemed to be exactly what one would expect to find atop a banker's desk– correspondence, records, and accounts of various kinds. A paper fell, and as I bent to pick it up, I noticed a loose panel on the side of the desk. I freed it from its place and found several folded letters tucked carefully inside. My breath caught.

I did not read them, not yet. There was no time. I shoved a couple of them into the bodice of my dress, returned the panel, and was back in my chair by the time Augustus returned, with a tray of tea for mother and me in hand, his expression untroubled.

Mother stared at me, pale and shaken, her hands clenched in her lap. Augustus resumed his seat, continuing as though nothing had occurred. But I could not remain for another moment. I sipped my tea twice and then stood up, unable to contain myself.

"I am so sorry to interrupt, Mr. Finch, but we must take our leave," I eyed Mother carefully.

Mother looked at me, surprise still evident on her face. "Bridget."

"Please," I said softly, meeting her gaze. "I am... feeling rather unwell."

Her bewildered expression offered no cover for my actions, and she hastily apologized to Augustus.

"But of course, m'lady, I do hope a good rest will help you recover promptly," he said with a slight bow of his head.

It wasn't until we were safely aboard the carriage that I felt like I could breathe again.

Mother turned on me at once, "Bridget, what you just did is absolutely,"

"I know," I said, interrupting her. "But I had to."

She stared at me, torn between fear, anger, and disbelief.

Pressed against my ribs, hidden beneath my gown, hopefully lay the proof of everything I suspected. I did not want to open them in front of her and have to explain everything, not yet anyways; I did not really know what the letters would reveal, and I wanted to tell her only once I had uncovered the full truth. She had to remain in the dark for now.

"Bridget, I demand an explanation for your complete lack of decency towards a man who was just trying to help us," Mother rebuked.

"Mother, I need you to trust me. Many things are happening beyond your sight at this time. Give me time, and all shall reveal itself soon enough." I pleaded. I felt slightly like William when he had asked me to trust him for withholding information. Asking for her trust in me caused me to wince. I justified it because, unlike William, I was promising to reveal the truth in due time.

The moment we stepped inside, I did not pause.

"I need a moment alone," I said, already moving toward the stairs.

"Bridget," Mother began.

"Please, Mother." I pleaded. Her quiet disapproval was evident in her face as she sighed, shut her eyes tightly, and waved me away.

I raced into my room and promptly shut the door behind me. I sat on the side of my bed, my hands trembling while I pulled the letters free. I briskly opened the first one, and I felt like my eyes could not read it fast enough. The handwriting was stark.

Mr. Augustus Finch,

I must speak with you on matters that have caused me to grow weary, and I do hope this letter finds you in a much better temper than the one I write to you in now.

For some time, I have felt my position within the business to be unstable and insecure. Agreements that were once spoken plainly now arrive delayed or not at all. Profits are accounted for without my sight, and my income is steadily decreasing. I do not care for it.
You assured me, when this venture began, that the three of us involved were equals. That trust would bind us where law could not. Has distance made it easier for you to forget such assurances?
My decisions are no longer considered with the weight they once held. I am a stranger within the enterprise I helped begin all those years ago.

Do not mistake my concern for disloyalty, but loyalty cannot survive long where it is not given in return.

Sincerely,

Señor Leonardo Rodríguez

I lowered the letter, disheartened that it did not bring me clarity, but only more questions. What was this business they had together? Surely it was not Finch Financial & Bank. A bank would not handle frequent shipments, would it? I also did not think Augustus had any business partners, so who was this Leonardo Rodriguez? His name was entirely unfamiliar to me. I went for the next letter, praying it would provide answers. As I unfolded the paper, I noticed the script was bold, a little difficult to decipher, and unmistakably my father's. I took a deep breath as I felt grief and anger twist within me.

Adder,

Leon's shipment was received on schedule. You will find that all is accounted for. No complications experienced upon receipt, although the harbor inspection ran longer than usual. We should consider using a different port of entry for the next shipment. Inventory as follows:

24 cases Port - Negus
15 cases Liqueur - Ratafia
17 cases Cognac- La Rochelle
32 cases Wine - Lion's Blood
12 cases Wine - Madeira - Sercial

All secured and will be distributed promptly and as agreed.
Payment tallies to be sent.

I stared at the words, my heart pounding so loudly I thought I might be ill. Jackal. James. Jackal was Father, León must be this Leonardo gentleman, and Adder must be Augustus; how fitting for him to be the snake—the one with the venom, or where my father's death was concerned, the poison. My hands involuntarily gripped the paper more firmly.

It was clear what they had been up to. Smuggling. The danger William wished to keep me from. The realization settled slowly. It explained everything—the way Father had been increasingly uneasy, the late nights, the whispered arguments between my parents I had never been meant to hear.

He had not simply been gambling. He had been funding it. Running goods through secret channels, skirting the law, profiting from it. And Augustus had been part of it, perhaps from the beginning. I found myself just staring at a particular listed product, Lion's Blood. The very item that had been the death of my father, he had helped smuggle into the country. The irony of it put my stomach into knots. The walls of the room suddenly felt too close, the air too still, as if the truth had taken up all the space in the room, leaving no room for me. I pressed the letters up into my sleeve and hurried outside, the cool air striking my face as I stepped onto the path.

I did not know where I meant to go. I only needed space to process the new information. The grounds stretched out before me, quiet in the late afternoon, a handful of workers moving about their tasks with steady familiarity. Gravel crunched beneath my hurried steps, my thoughts racing faster than my feet could carry me.

Someone called my name, but I barely registered it until a hand closed gently, but firmly, around my arm.

"Miss—"

It was Antonio. He stepped into my path, his brow furrowed as he took in my face. I must have had a rather dishevelled appearance.

"You should not be out like this," he said softly. "You look unwell."

"I am fine," I insisted, though my voice betrayed me.

He did not argue. Instead, he guided me with a careful strength toward the fountain just off the path, his arm offering a soft support as if to convey his fear I might fall if he let me go. I did feel rather unsteady.

"Sit here," he suggested.

I sank onto the stone, the cool surface grounding me back into the present moment. For a time, neither of us spoke. The gentle sound of running water filled the silence; my breath became less frantic and steadier as I took in my surroundings.

Antonio took a seat next to me, concern covering his eyes, "What has happened?" he implored. I hesitated, then pulled the letters from my sleeve, my fingers trembling as I handed them to him.

"I found these," I said. "Hidden in Mr. Finch's office."

He slowly unfolded the first page and scanned it intently. The color drained from his face. For a moment, it seemed as if he did not breathe; he did not even move—only stared, as though the words had struck him incapable.

"What is the matter?" I asked, my voice barely above a whisper. Antonio did not answer at once. I noticed his jaw clenched shut as he seemed to contemplate something with great urgency.

"Antonio?" I said quietly, the change in his face unsettling me more than the letters themselves. "Are you quite all right?"

He wiped sweat off his face with his sleeve, and his movements became more controlled.

"I—yes," he said, though his voice lacked its usual confidence. "It is nothing. Only surprising."

Before I could inquire any further, a loud voice cut across the grounds.

"Mr.Rodriguez! We are not paid to dawdle. You have many tasks to complete before we light the lanterns for the night." The head groundskeeper, Mr. Blythe, strode toward us with obvious irritation.

Rodriguez? I glanced at Antonio as the name landed like a stone in my chest. He rose at once, leaving the letters on the stone next to me, his movements slower now, as though weighed down by something unseen.

"Yes, sir," he said quietly. His eyes met mine before he turned away. For a moment, neither of us spoke.

Rodriguez. *Leonardo* Rodriguez. The name echoed through my mind as the connection formed. Antonio had spoken briefly of his father's illness and his mother's passing years ago, but he had never revealed anything more specific. No names, not even his own surname, only small bits of information. I had thought nothing of it until now. Antonio Rodriguez.

He hesitated, just briefly, as though wanting to say something, then lowered his gaze and walked back toward the lawn. I watched him go, confusion tightening further in my chest.

He looked sad. Not frightened or guilty, just sad. And I could not decide which troubled me more.

Chapter Ten: Revelations

I glided back to the cottage in a strange haze as it felt like my feet were carrying me there without my commanding them to do so. My thoughts churned, and I felt as if I could scarcely tell which way was forward. Antonio was related to Leonardo. Leonardo was a business partner with Father and Augustus, and they were smugglers. Leonardo was unhappy with them. But why was Antonio here? Was Leonardo here as well? Some of what Antonio had told me about himself was true, and that his father really was ill, and Antonio was here in his place. But in his place to do what, exactly? My mind raced with questions that I had no answers to, yet again.

By the time I reached the house, my breath was unsteady, my hands cold despite the mild air. I entered through the servant's door without thinking—it was simply the nearest, and I had no patience left for propriety.

The kitchen was empty. No clatter of dishes, no low conversation, no sign of Jane or Mr. Smith. Only the faint warmth of the stove and the quiet hum of a house mid-afternoon. And there, on the wooden table near the hearth, sat a bottle of wine. I stopped short. Even from across the room, I knew it. The crest was unmistakable—a lion reared, emboldened into the dark green glass.

Lion's Blood. The wine that had been received and dispersed by my father, according to his shipment record, which I found just this morning. I grabbed the bottle; the glass was thick and heavy, and it was only about halfway full. The crest was identical to the one on the shard I had held only days before. How had it come here? I moved quickly toward the front room with the bottle in hand.

Mother and Jane were speaking softly as Mother was ruminating over her afternoon tea, and Jane was busy cleaning the fireplace. Both looked up as I entered, but whatever greeting they meant to offer died at the sight of my face.

"Jane," I said, my voice strained despite my effort to steady it, "where did this come from?"

Jane blinked, startled, her gaze darting between me and the bottle.

"I—well, miss, I couldn't say for certain," she began, attempting a weak smile. "Mr. Smith does enjoy a drink now and again. I assumed—"

"Assumptions will not do," Mother cut in sharply. She and I both knew Mr. Smith too well to know he did not partake of alcoholic beverages, except for a Sherry from time to time on very special occasions—a fact Jane seemed to have forgotten in her short time on staff. Jane startled at once as she wiped her hands clean on her apron.

Mother's posture straightened as she said, "Do not attempt to placate us with guesses, Jane. My daughter is in the throes of something immensely important, and I will not have the truth buried beneath convenience. Not when she won't even confide in me about it," I could almost feel the hurt in her voice. I looked down at the floorboards, slightly ashamed of leaving her in the dark.

"Tell us plainly, my dear," Mother continued, "where did that bottle come from?"

Jane pursed her lips as if she were trying to think of a different excuse, but she let out a large sigh instead. "It was one of the groundskeepers," she admitted. "The day you and Miss Bridget went for tea at the Finches'. He came by, only briefly. He had the bottle with him and said he wished to share a glass. He was very kind about it. Poured some for me himself."

My heart hammered.

"And you allowed him inside?"

Jane nodded, her cheeks flushing. "Only into the front room. It seemed harmless. I thought nothing of it. He is such a kind man, you must believe me."

"So this was not your first interaction with him?" I implored, an anger stewing within me.

"Oh no, Miss. We have been friends for some months now, actually. We met in town one day. I was purchasing something for Lady Rosamund when he overheard me speak of the Hartwoods. We bonded over the fact that he, too, is on staff for a member of the Hartwood family, Lady Charlotte, of course." Jane must have noticed my mouth drop open and my brow furrow. "But I didn't think of him as a person of questionable character, Miss. He has always been so respectable."

It was becoming near impossible to hide my surprise, "This was in fact the same impression I had of him when I first made his acquaintance as well, but things are not always as they first appear," I retorted, "Jane, how close were you with him? Tell me, did you disclose information to him about the wine bottle shard I kept on my vanity?"

There was a pause as Jane thought. "I am ashamed to say that yes, I did tell him about it, the day after I discovered it on your person, we had met along the road to Ashcombe, and I confided in him of my new position at the cottage, how sad it was to witness such grief, and how peculiar you were acting in particular, Miss Bridget. It was then that I told him how odd it was to find the wine shard in your dress and how peculiar it was that you did not want to dispose of it."

So Antonio knew about the shard long before I had even told him about it myself. He must have pieced together that I would eventually conclude that Father's death was not accidental, and schemed to retrieve the shard himself, but I had to be sure.

"Were you with him the entire time?" I asked quickly.

"Pardon, Miss, but what time are you referring to?" she asked carefully, treading carefully as if she were walking on glass.

"The day he came to see you here at the cottage. Was he in your presence the entire time he was here?"

Jane's eyes dropped, "No… not the whole time."

My breath caught, "What do you mean?"

"I remembered the kettle," she said, her voice smaller now, realizing she had made a rather large mistake. "I had left tea on the stove, and it began to whistle. I stepped away only a moment, just long enough to tend to it, and also to prepare us some bread and cheese to have with the wine. When I returned, he was still there. We finished our conversation, and then he left."

"Was it Antonio?" I asked, the name coming out harsher than I intended.

Jane looked up at me suddenly, as if it was strange that I had known his name. Her reaction was enough of an answer.

"I… I don't want any trouble, miss," she blubbered, "please, I…"

"Jane," Mother soothed, attempting to get the information from her, "We require an answer."

"Yes," Jane cricd, "Yes, it was Antonio."

Antonio had been alone in the house the day the shard disappeared. My mind raced backward—Leonardo's letter, the business, the resentment woven through every line. Antonio's reaction to the letter at the fountain. The sadness in his face when his name was spoken.

It all began to unfold further. He had a motive. He had access. He had reason to hate the men who had built their fortunes alongside his father and who were supposedly attempting to cut him off. And he had been close—close enough to me, to this house, to my trust.

Antonio had taken the evidence- the wine shard, but with that, he had made a mistake, bringing another one of the Lion's Blood bottles to the cottage, thinking either I would never see it, or forgetting to take it with him when he left. He must have been the one to steal the whole case from the Stag and Crown.

My grip tightened around the bottle, the lion crest digging into my palm.

Antonio—who had listened to me, comforted me, and walked beside me in my grief.

Antonio—whose father had been bound to mine in secret dealings and quiet resentment.

Antonio— who, I realized with a sickening certainty, had likely killed my father.

Chapter Eleven:

The Road to Ashcombe

I felt betrayed, taken advantage of, and I felt sick to my stomach. I could not remain in the cottage a minute longer, so I dashed out the front door in a rush of fury that carried me down the lane before any sense had a chance to catch up with me. I gathered my skirts in my hands and began to run as quickly as I could. There was no time to wait for a carriage to arrive. No time to explain to anyone what I now knew. I heard Mother call after me, but the determination in my step left no room for stopping.

As I ran, the cold air filled my lungs, the graveled road felt unsteady beneath my shoes, and my heart seemed to beat in unison with my hurried pace. I made my way past the Hartwood Estate and was heading down the road towards Ashcombe. There was only one person on my mind: Antonio. He would most likely know by now. He must. The letters, the questions, the look on my face when Mr. Blythe spoke his name— If he had any sense, he would already be on his way out of the county, slipping quietly into the same shadows from which he had come.

So I ran faster, and my mind seemed to race along with me; memories began to fill in the gaps and answer questions I had been turmoiling over. How could I have been so naive? I had been too blind, and too willing perhaps, to overlook the signs. The morning after Father's death, I had strolled into the gardens, where I accidentally met Antonio. He had been there working in the flower beds, kneeling in the dirt in the same area where I later found the wine bottle shard streaked with blood. His blood. No doubt, he was attempting to clean up other shards that remained in the same general area, and happened to miss the one near my feet. I had thought him dutiful, conscientious. Now I saw it for what it was: a man retracing his steps, desperate to erase them.

Then there was his eagerness to guide my suspicions elsewhere. How quickly he had agreed that Mr. Finch seemed troubled. How readily he suggested confusion, accident, or misfortune. Anything to keep my thoughts focused on Mr. Finch rather than suspecting him.

My lungs burned, but I did not slow.

Rupert's account surfaced next. A figure leaving the grounds quickly the night of Father's death, heading down the road unsteadily, hurriedly, disappearing into the darkness of the trees beyond. I had pictured Augustus, but it now seemed entirely impossible for him to have both left the grounds quickly (his portly frame did not allow for hastened movement) and, not long after, leave the party with his family, wishing us his utmost regrets with tear-filled eyes. But Antonio worked the grounds. This would account for his familiarity with them. He would know how to vanish promptly without notice. He just hadn't accounted for Rupert.

And then there were the letters. The way his face had drained of color when he read what I now believe to be his own father's words. The name the head groundskeeper had used to address Antonio was the same name signed at the bottom of the letter—Rodriguez. There had been no hiding it at that moment. No easy charm, no careful redirection. Only shock and something deeper. Grief. Resentment. History I had never meant to see. My lungs ached from the sharp cold air.

All the signs had been there, laid plainly before me. And still I had trusted him, confided in him. I had let myself believe that his kindness was simple, uncalculated, and genuine. The lane dipped slightly ahead as Ashcombe came into view afar off. I forced my legs onward despite how heavy they were beginning to feel. If he was running, I would find him. If what I had surmised really was true, if Antonio Rodriguez had befriended me, led me to believe he fancied me, all while knowing he had taken my father's life, then I would hear it from his own mouth.

The lane opened ahead, bending toward Ashcombe, and there, just beyond the hedgerow, I saw him. He was walking quickly, his shoulders set, a satchel slung across his back as though he meant to escape quickly and quietly. He had not yet seen me.

"Antonio!" My voice tore from my throat, raw and tired. He stopped at once, turning, surprise flashing across his face as I closed the distance between us, breathless, furious, shaking with more than the effort of the run. I slowed to a stop as I approached him.

"Why did you do it?" I demanded. The question seemed to hang in the air between us as he stood there with a great dread on his face. He watched me attempt to catch my breath.

His posture slumped slightly, and a painful look crossed his face. He lowered his head for a moment, squinted his eyes shut as though the accusation had struck deeply. When he looked back at me, there was no denial in his eyes. No outrage. No attempt to flee. Only sadness. Deep, steady, and unmistakable.

"I wondered when you would see it," he said at last, his voice low, roughened at the edges. "I just hoped not to be here when you found out." He drew a slow breath, as though steadying himself before stepping somewhere he could not return from.

"Tell me what happened," I implored.

He could not meet my eye; rather, he stared at his shoes as he began, "My father believed they were stealing from him," he said quietly. "From his share of the profits. It began about a year ago. The shipments were the same, the same quantity, the same routes, but the money that reached him grew smaller each time. At first, he thought it was an error. Then carelessness. But it did not stop." His eyes shifted up and past me, toward the road, as if the memory itself stood there waiting.

"He is not a man given to imagination," he continued. "Nor to weakness. He would have made the journey to England to handle things himself if he could, but his health has been failing him for years now, so he sent me instead."

"He sent you to spy," I said bitterly.

"More to observe," he corrected, "and to learn what I could without causing James or Augustus to know of his suspicions. He did not ask for revenge, only truth. If I were able to uncover that they were stealing from him, he could confront them about it, but if his suspicions had no evidence to support them, then he would leave the matter alone, and I would return home."

"So you came here," I said, my throat felt tight, "to Hartwood."

“Yes,” he said as he ran a hand through his hair. He seemed anxious in a way I had not seen him act before.

“My father had worked these grounds once, long before I was born,” he said. “Head groundskeeper, actually. It was here in the gardens that he had overheard your father and Augustus share many a private conversation as he worked quietly. One day, he politely interjected into one of their conversations and carefully proposed smuggling to them. My father grew up working the vineyards in Spain and already had connections in the business. It seemed an opportune moment, with your father’s gambling debts becoming too much, and Augustus not knowing how to help him. He said your father was on the brink of such sorrow that he was contemplating ending his own life. His desperation made my father confident in suggesting this illegal activity as a solution for his problems, and his plan was quite welcome,” Antonio trailed off, as if he felt guilty for exposing parts of my father that would be painful for me to hear.

He continued, "My father wrote me a letter of recommendation to Lady Charlotte. He spoke of the estate and the work he accomplished here for years. Naturally, she remembered him, and it was enough for her to hire me without question.”

Its simplicity made my stomach turn.

“I watched James,” he said. “And Augustus. My father was right; they would frequently meet in Charlotte's gardens to discuss these matters. Of course, it took many months of attempted observations to learn of the shipments arriving, the accounts being kept, and what was not being kept. I wrote to my father whenever I could to tell him about what I was seeing.”

"And what did you see?" I demanded, feeling a strong urge to defend my father, even though he was not quite the honest man he should have been.

His eyes met mine again, steady, unflinching now.

"I saw that your father was not the man he had once been," Antonio said. "His drinking grew worse. The gambling even more so. The money that should have been accounted for vanished. And Augustus—" He hesitated. "Augustus knew and tried to stop his friend, but things had grown beyond even his capability of rescuing."

I felt great shame and sorrow for the life my father had chosen to live. I cast my eyes down to the dirt as Antonio continued. "When I first came here, I had no intention of anyone getting hurt, but it all came to a head when I observed your father late one night gambling at The Stag and Crown. It seemed as if no amount of alcohol in the world could satisfy his need to drown his worries. He was speaking boisterously, and the other gentlemen in the circle gave more than a few comments about how they doubted he could pay for his losses. He was so bold and drunk as to admit that he had foreign ventures others knew nothing about and that all would be paid in full. Your father's carelessness was on the verge of exposing the business my father had so carefully built up. I couldn't have it all blow up just because James couldn't control his distasteful habits. Who's to say he wouldn't even reveal my father's name and get him sent to prison? My father's health is so poor that he would die in the first few weeks of being detained."

"And you took matters into your own hands," I said.

His look hardened. "I came for answers," he replied. "But answers are not always given freely. It was at this point that I decided to keep my father in the dark. I did not want a paper trail with proof of my motive or my plans to take your father out of the equation, so my letters to him remained vague."

There was something in his voice then—something darker, tied down with regret—that made my pulse falter.

"So you decided to poison him," I said starkly.

He raised his eyebrows in surprise at my knowledge of his doings, then closed his eyes briefly, as though the memory itself was difficult to face. He exhaled slowly, the sound thin in the quiet between us.

"I took the wine from the Stag and Crown the week prior," he said. "A whole case. It was common enough that I hoped no one would question its absence. I prepared it. Laced it with a poison that would not act at once to allow for time to leave the scene and avoid suspicion. I was unsure how I would get him to drink it, though, but I knew Lady Charlotte was holding a ball soon, and figured that might be the easiest time for him to drink something unknowingly."

I imagined him taking his time concluding that he needed to kill my father, and how he so carefully planned how to do it; I felt shivers run up and down my spine.

"I did not want it to look like murder," he continued. "If it looked like an accident, a drunken fall, it would be something no one would question."

I could not hide my disdain, nor the discomfort it made me feel to hear his story, but I felt a pressing need to hear the truth, so I listened quietly as he continued.

"I waited in the gardens the night of the ball," he said, his voice distant, as though he were speaking from somewhere far behind himself. "Sure enough, James showed up with a bottle of brandy in hand. He was pacing back and forth along the path, muttering to himself. I could not make out the words, only the anger in them."

Antonio swallowed, his voice growing quiet.

"I did not want to be seen," he continued. "Every instinct told me to stay hidden. But I had come too far, and my father's health was failing more with each letter. I could not stand by and watch James destroy everything while my father suffered for it."

He rubbed a hand over his face, as though the memory still weighed heavily on him.

"James set the bottle down on the stone ledge and continued pacing. He did not even notice where he left it. So I moved. Quietly. Quickly. I took the brandy and left the wine in its place without him noticing."

My breath caught, "So you swapped them when he was not looking," I said under my breath.

Antonio nodded, "I had to take any chance that came my way. I took the chance to save what remained for my father." He peered past my shoulder as though that night was still unfolding in front of him.

"Not long after, Augustus appeared," Antonio continued. "He had come looking for James. They began arguing almost at once. I could not hear every word, but enough to understand."

My heart pounded.

"Augustus was uneasy," he said. "He admitted he did not feel right about skimming from my father's share and using it to cover James's debts. He said it could not continue. That it would ruin them all if it came to light. James did not take it well," Antonio went on quietly. "He grew angrier and accused Augustus of betrayal and cowardice. Said he would handle his affairs as he pleased."

Antonio's voice lowered.

"James picked up the wine then. Drank from it without looking. Once, and then twice. Then he stopped and looked at the bottle as though something about it displeased him. I saw him glance around in search of his brandy, but obviously, he could not find it."

The image formed sharply in my mind.

"And then he smashed it," Antonio said. "He smashed the wine bottle against the stones, and the glass broke and went everywhere.

I grimaced as I recalled times when Father had become unyieldingly angry, but I had never seen him become destructive like that before.

Antonio carried on, "Augustus took several steps back. The somewhat violent behavior seemed to shock him. I could tell he did not want a scene. He told James they would speak again once his wits had returned, and then he left."

By now, my body had regained its composure from the run, but I still felt my hands trembling. The sweat on my brow chilled me as a cold autumnal wind gently blew against it.

"A few minutes passed," Antonio said, his voice growing thinner and thinner, as though each word cost him something. "The argument burned itself out. James stood there a moment longer, breathing hard, then attempted to steady himself. He straightened his coat and headed back toward the house."

I held my breath.

"I knew what would happen next," he continued. "The poison would not wait long. He would grow weak, unsteady, and then collapse. And if it happened without explanation," He shook his head. "People would question it. Look closer."

His hands flexed at his sides, as though remembering a pain.

"I panicked," he admitted. "I was not thinking straight, and it seemed necessary that the glass be near him so that when they found his body, the shattered bottle would leave no doubt that it was a drunken fall, nothing more."

The words struck like ice.

"So I gathered the pieces," he said. "As quickly as I could. The larger shards first. My hands—" He paused, glancing down at them. "I cut them badly. I hardly noticed at the time, my urgency seemed to beat at the forefront of my mind like a battle drum."

He removed his gloved hands to show the scars that were covering his hands; some of the wounds were still healing. I realized that I had never had an interaction with him where his gloves were not on. Even when he had grabbed my hand and kissed it softly, the gloves were on. I merely thought this was because he worked on the grounds, but it was to conceal evidence proving his guilt.

"I followed him toward the steps," Antonio went on, his voice rough. "Trying to move what I could. But it was dark. The lanterns were dim, and I knew, even then, that I had missed pieces. I could not see them all."

The image flashed in my mind: broken glass scattered in the garden, the bloody shard I had found.

"He fell soon after," Antonio said quietly, tears beginning to fill his eyes. "I heard it. The sound of it. And I knew it was finished, and that my father would be safe. Augustus would be a fair business partner to him without James around."

A long silence stretched between us.

"I did not stay," he added. "I could not chance being seen anywhere near his person, but I knew there was still broken glass left behind. So I decided to return at first light and finish clearing the scene of the pieces I had missed." Antonio's shoulders sagged as if the weight of the memory was settling fully over him now.

"My plan felt simple after that," he admitted. "Finish gathering what shards remained… and leave and return home to my father in Spain. That was always the plan."

He hesitated, then shook his head faintly.

"But leaving at once would have drawn attention. A man vanishing immediately after someone's death? Someone would have questioned it. Even if they believed it was an accident."

He exhaled slowly.

"So I told myself I would stay a fortnight, long enough that no one would suspect. Then I would go, say my father needed me, that his health had worsened, and that I was called home to care for him."

His voice faltered then, something softer breaking through. He paused for a long time before speaking again. I felt as if I had no words to fill the void.

"That was before I met you."

The words landed gently with a sorrowful tone.

"I did not expect…" He searched for the right phrasing, his head drooping. "I did not expect James to have a daughter like you. Nor did I expect myself to…" He stopped, then began again, quieter. "To regret what I had done."

He looked at me fully then, and there was no calculation in his expression now—only a raw, unguarded pain.

"I told myself it was necessary," he said. "That I was protecting my father. That James had brought it upon himself. But each day after, each time I saw you grieving, each time you spoke to me with kindness I had not earned…"

His fists clenched.

"I have carried it since," he admitted. "The knowledge that I caused you to suffer. That I stood beside you, listened to you, and said nothing."

The silence stretched between us, heavy and aching.

"I never meant to hurt you," he said finally, his voice rough. "That is the truth I cannot escape. Whatever I did, whatever I believed I had to do, I did not expect to meet you. And I did not expect it to matter. I also did not expect you to be so keenly astute. I was completely frightened the day Jane told me you had found a shard of glass in the gardens and that you were acting strangely. I did everything in my power to keep you from suspecting me, but I knew I had to obtain the shard of glass from your possession." He continued with urgency in his voice, as if trying to convince me that his actions had been honorable, that his feelings for me and the regret that followed somehow negated his wrongdoing.

"I used my friendship with your lady's maid, Jane, in hopes that she would reveal where the shard was, if it had been disposed of, or maybe even bring it to me herself. It felt like time was closing in on me, though, and so I waited for a time when you and your mother left by carriage somewhere. I saw my chance a few days after your father's death when I was trimming the main lawn. Both you and your mother left, and Mr. Smith had gone to the village. I quickly snuck away from my duties and grabbed a bottle of wine to share with Miss Jane. To my surprise and luck, she let me in promptly and, without even noticing, gave me time to search the rooms for the shard as she prepared food in the kitchen. I quickly found it atop the vanity in your room."

Antonio's voice shifted again, something harder moving beneath the sorrow.

"I had hoped the shard would be the end of it," he said. "That once it disappeared, your questions would stop. That grief would take its place, and you would move on."

A chill crept through me yet again.

"But you did not," he went on, a quiet anger entering his tone, "You kept searching. Kept looking. And now..." His voice faltered slightly. "Now you know everything."

His confession settled between us like rocks at the bottom of a landslide.

"What is your plan now?" I asked, stepping back slightly, hoping he wouldn't notice the distance I was trying to place between us.

"Miss Hartwood... Bridget," he implored, "come with me."

"I beg your pardon?" I did not think my being was capable of feeling any more confusion than it did at this moment.

"You cannot stay here," he said suddenly, stepping closer. "You understand what this means. You know what I have done."

I stared at him, unable to speak.

"Come with me," Antonio urged, his voice softening, coaxing. "Leave this place. Leave all of it. Leave behind the grief and the painful memories. Your father was not the man you believed him to be. He gambled away your future, endangered your mother, and cared more for his vices than for either of you. He's left you with nothing. There is nothing for you here. I implore you, come with me, and I will care for you. I promise there is happiness beyond this place, beyond this loss."

I stepped back once more, repulsed by his offer.

"Do not," I said, my voice sounded shaky, "speak as if you truly knew my father. He may not have been the man he ought to have been, and was riddled with bad habits, but at least he was not a murderer."

My tone was accusational and harsh, and seemed to hurt him more than the cuts on his hands did. He suddenly reached his hands out and closed them around mine. Desperation filled his voice.

"You must come," he insisted. "You are the only one who knows the truth; you are the only one who can destroy me. And I cannot allow that, not after everything. You have to understand what I did; I did it for my father out of love. I must see him again, or it will all have been for naught."

For a single, disorienting moment, I faltered. His voice was low, persuasive. His eyes were intent, pleading, familiar in a way that made my resolve waver. There had been kindness there once. Warmth. A strength I had trusted and leaned on throughout my despair. For the briefest heartbeat, I almost considered it. Then my tear-filled eyes dropped to his hands that were gently wrapped around mine.

They were still marked with thin, jagged cuts crossing his knuckles and palms, some barely healed, others raw, the unmistakable wounds of someone who had handled broken glass in haste and darkness. The image of him frantically collecting the glass and throwing it next to my father's corpse flashed across my mind like a bolt of lightning. I felt a strong panic surge through me as I pulled hard against his strong grip.

"Let me go!" I demanded.

But his demeanor turned from pleading to anger in an instant, and his hold on me only tightened.

Chapter Twelve:

A Change of Heart

There was a brisk chill in the morning breeze that I did not care for. The weather of the past few weeks had slowly been a testament to the beginning of Autumn, which meant winter would arrive in only a few short months, and I would not be able to enjoy riding like this until Spring began to show. It had been a long ride this morning, and my face felt cold from the wind against it. Wallace rode to my left, and Colin was just ahead. Their typical easy conversation seemed to rise and fall with the rhythm of the horses' steps. It was a morning I might have ordinarily called invigorating, but today I found I simply could not.

My thoughts refused the present entirely, circling instead around one person, one face, one look I had not been able to shake since the funeral.

Bridget.

I had known her displeasure before. We had quarrelled as children, as friends do, over trifles that seemed enormous at the time. But this was different. There had been hurt in her eyes, and beneath it, something I despised to admit looked like distrust. The knowledge sat ill with me.

I pressed my heels lightly to my horse, letting him move a little ahead of the others, though I heard Wallace say something about the state of the road and Colin laugh in reply. Typically, I would have joined them, but today, their words passed through me without purchase.

I could not blame her. I had warned her the night of her father's death, then withdrawn. Spoken in half-truths, refused explanation when she had most needed one. To her, it must seem like cowardice and betrayal.

And yet the truth was not mine alone to tell. Nor was it safe to place upon her shoulders, not when I scarcely understood its full shape myself.

Still, I hated it. Hated the thought that she believed me indifferent. That she might think I had abandoned her in her grief, when in truth it had taken every restraint I possessed to leave her.

Wallace drew level with me then, casting a glance my way.

"You've not said a word this past hour," he remarked lightly. "Either the ride displeases you, or your thoughts are elsewhere."

I managed a faint smile. "You are quite the astute gentleman, Wallace."

Colin reined in slightly, turning in his saddle. "Still in knots over Miss Hartwood, are you? Miss Isabelle's attempts at capturing your attention seem to bear her no fruit," he teased.

I did not answer at once, which was answer enough. The two exchanged a look, one of those silent understandings born of long acquaintance.

"You've made a hash of it, whatever it is," Colin added, lightly.

I exhaled slowly.

"She has reason to be angry," I said at last. "More reason than I care to admit."

Wallace studied me for a moment, his expression losing its teasing edge. "And yet you ride instead of setting it right."

"If it were mine to set right," I replied quietly, "I would have done so already."

The words lingered between us, heavier than I intended.

"Well, if it were me," Colin mused, "and I was this taken up with a young lady, I would do whatever it took to mend things. It's not often we have the chance to enter into a marriage with someone that we already know we feel strongly for."

"Colin, since when did you start making sense?" I jabbed.

"Don't listen to him, he's just trying to lure you away from Miss Isabelle so he can have her and all her riches for himself," Wallace said as he rode his horse close to Colin's and pushed his shoulder, smiling.

They began to banter and bicker like children and hardly noticed when my speed increased as I headed into town towards Father's office. I kept thinking I could not set things right with Bridget without telling her the whole truth, about my Father's illegal business, about how he wanted me to become a part of it, and how I played along reluctantly. I did not want to live a lie as Father had been doing with me all these years, but I needed to set aside whatever fear of consequence was holding me back from confronting him so that I could be with Bridget, if she would have me. Colin was right, though, I ought to do whatever it takes to change her mind.

By the time I reached the outskirts of town, I could no longer bear the company of my own thoughts. I turned toward the corral just beyond the main road. The groom looked up in mild surprise as I dismounted, but I gave him no time for questions, pressing the reins into his hands and steadying the animal with a firm pat before striding away.

The sign above the door read, in clean black lettering edged with gold: Finch Financial & Bank. I pushed open the creaky door and stepped inside. The familiar scent of musty leather, ink, and old paper greeted me immediately. To me, it was the smell of order, industry, and my father's success. It had always been a place of reassurance to me growing up. Today, it felt suffocating.

I moved quickly through the front room, past clerks who looked up at my entrance with polite surprise, and toward the back office. My father's door stood closed.

I pushed the door open abruptly, fearing that if I knocked and waited for his reply, I would lose all sense of confidence to accomplish what I needed to.

There sat my father, Mr. Augustus Finch, alone in his office, reviewing ledgers and letters. He looked up from his desk, a little startled, "William?" he asked.

"I want no part in it," I said at once, the words spewing out of me as if they had been held back by a dam for several months.

He breathed in deeply, his brow furrowed, "No part in what exactly, son?"

"In your dishonesty, your disregard for the law, your secrets… I want no part in it. I intended to lead my life on in the financial business you have taught me, but whatever dark means you and James Hartwood have used to gain this success, I want no part in it."

A silence fell upon the room, and a sadness crept across Father's face.

He set his book down slowly as he replied, "You misunderstand…"

"No," I interrupted, feeling a rising frustration come forth, "I understand quite perfectly, and I feel I cannot be clearer of my shame for how you have conducted yourself in your business. Here you have been living in such a way that contradicts the very teachings you have always taught me to uphold." My voice came out bold and strong, which made any hesitation between comments that much more stark.

"I believed you to be an honest man," I continued, "I have always admired you, respected you. I thought everything you built came through diligence and integrity. To learn that your life, our family's life, was intertwined with something so… so disreputable." I shook my head, unable to finish.

"I will not be part of it," I said again, more quietly now. "I will not build my future upon secrets and deceit. I would rather begin with nothing."

Father did not speak at once. The confusion had left his face, replaced by something far more painful… sorrow. He leaned back in his chair slowly, his gaze dropping to the desk before him.

"You think I am proud of it," he said at last, his voice low.

I was unprepared for his somber reaction. I had expected him to yell; I had expected him to be upset that I would not share in his ventures. I thought he would disown me entirely. His regretful countenance and his sadness struck me harder than any anger could have.

"I did what I believed necessary," he went on. "For our family. For a dear friend's survival. The world is not kind to men who begin with nothing, William. Respectability is often built upon choices we would rather not name aloud."

"I wish to be a trustworthy man," I replied, "you have taught me about this banking industry, that's what I have been preparing for, not… not smuggling. Even if I have to live a modest life, I will at least be able to live with myself, instead of dealing with someone involved in such depravity as theft and murder," I explained.

"Murder?" Father scooted back his chair and rose to his feet, "What are you accusing me of, boy?"

"I'm not accusing you of anything, but merely questioning that if the smuggling business was not in existence, would Lord Hartwood still be alive today?"

Father dabbed his kerchief on his eye, trying to keep a tear from falling down his cheek as he spoke, "Now that, there is no way of knowing what might have been."

There was a sudden knock on the door.

"Yes?" Father replied. His secretary opened the door, letter in hand.

"Sorry, sir. This letter just arrived for you," she said as she placed the letter on his desk.

"Thank you, Miss Giles, you may go now," he entreated as he sat back in his chair, defeated, and the door shut once again.

"We created the smuggling business entirely for James. His gambling debts had amounted so greatly that he was about to lose everything. The man was nearly suicidal. A Spaniard approached us with a business venture; he would obtain the tipple, ship it to us, and we would sell it. It was James's last hope, so I played along and have been playing along this whole time, even though it's been decades since it all began. But I have not spent a single farthing that has come to me from the smuggling. There have been times I have been tempted, but I always grow sick to my stomach when I think of it. So it has been accumulating in an account, untouched for these many years. James, however, managed to pay off all of his debts fairly quickly, but his gambling habits kept creeping back. He was unable to keep up with Ashcombe Park and the creditors demanding payments, even with the smuggling enterprise we had built. He began, unbeknownst to me, to skim off the Spaniard's payments. When I noticed the discrepancy, he said Leonardo was too old to notice.

"I confronted him about it the night of Charlotte's ball, saying it didn't feel right. This made James furious. I had planned the next day to see where his accounts were, how much he owed, and to use the money I had saved to pay off whatever debts he had, but that night he… he…" his head dropped down into his hands.

I was seeing my father in a new light. Regret filled my being; although I still did not approve of the illegal activity, it had been an effort to save his friend.

"James is gone now," I stated carefully as I sat in the chair across from him, "perhaps it is time to let the business go along with him."

There was a long pause as he processed. He finally lifted his head and decided, "You are right, son, it is time to put this evil behind us, though I am not sure how Leonardo will take the news; he has been a trustworthy man in all this, but this business has been his entire livelihood." His eyes flicked back to the letter recently laid atop his desk. “Perhaps we will discover something in this,” he said as he grabbed it, opened it, and read it aloud.

Mr. Augustus Finch,

It is with a troubled mind that I write to you, and I ask at the outset for your patience—and, if it can be given, your forgiveness.

You may already suspect the truth of what I am about to confess.
But I must inform you that many months ago, I sent my son, Antonio, to England with instructions to observe matters there and learn what he could of the business. I feared that my payments were being reduced for nefarious reasons, and asked him to find out what he could before confronting you and James about the matter. My health, as you know, has declined considerably over the past few years, so I could not travel myself, but I could not bear the thought of being tricked in such a way.

I did not send him in malice, however, nor with the intent to disrupt what we had built together. Only to understand.

He wrote to me at first with regularity. He spoke of the position he had secured on the groundskeeping staff at the Hartwood Estate. He sounded cautious at first, but determined. He spoke most often of a great dislike for James. He believed him to be reckless with both money and responsibility, an untrustworthy man. I urged patience and restraint, as I knew these things about James when we first started this venture years ago, but now Antonio's letters have ceased.

I have written again and again, with no reply. Months have now passed. My strength fails me more each day, and I find myself haunted by the fear that I have sent my son into something I can no longer reach, nor protect him from.

I do not know what he has learned, nor what conclusions he has drawn. Only that he is alone, and silent, and that I am no longer certain I shall live long enough to see him return without help.

If any loyalty remains between us, Augustus, I beg it of you now.
Find him. I ask not as a business partner, but as a father whose time is running short.

Tell him his home waits for him. Tell him I ask nothing more than his return.

And if my actions have offended—if sending him in secrecy has strained what trust remained between us—then I ask your pardon for that as well. Age and illness make men fearful, and you and I both know how fearful men make poor decisions.
I pray this letter reaches you swiftly, and that you might offer whatever aid you can.

Leonardo Rodriguez

I watched the color drain slowly from Father's face as his eyes moved back across the final lines.

"He has not heard from the boy in weeks," I contemplated aloud.

Father lowered the letter, staring into the distance beyond for what felt like a long moment.

"Antonio Rodriguez," he murmured. "Groundskeeper at Hartwood, just like his father."

The news hung heavily in the dark of the office.

"He suspected James," I said with a great dread, "Leonardo writes that much. That he believed James was reckless."

"And if he believed James was the source of his father's losses…" Father replied, his voice faltering.

A young man, sent by his ill father to observe in secret, as he notices carelessness and James' disregard for honesty, his resentment must have grown.

"And James is dead," I said at last.

Father looked at me then, something like horror dawning in his expression. "You think the boy—"

"I do not know what I think," I cut in, though my heart was already racing ahead of reason. "But I know this: Leonardo has not heard from him. And Antonio, for whatever reason, remains here."

My thoughts raced, and suddenly, a memory surged forward. It was Bridget at the graveside, the day of her father's funeral. Her voice was low and wounded.

"I have found more support and comfort from my maid and a lowly groundskeeper than I have from you," she had said.

A groundskeeper. My stomach turned. Antonio. I had not asked his name then. I had been too consumed by my own restraint, my own useless warnings, to think it important. But she had spoken of him with trust.

"It cannot be him," I said under my breath, though I felt the truth pressing in from all sides. "It cannot."

Father stood abruptly, the chair scraping behind him. "If the boy believed James was cheating his father—"

"He might have acted," I finished.

And Bridget had been searching. Asking questions. If she had confided in him, if she had told him of her suspicions…

"She knows," I uttered. "Or she suspects."

Father's head snapped toward me. "What do you mean?"

But I was already moving. I did not wait to explain. I did not wait for permission. I turned and strode from the office, the sound of my boots sharp against the wooden floor, ignoring the startled looks of the clerks as I passed. The musty air of the bank felt suffocating now, intolerable.

Antonio had a motive. Antonio had access. And Bridget had admitted to confiding in him.

I burst out into the street, the sunlight too bright, the air too thin. My pulse thundered in my ears as I ran towards the corral.

"Quickly," I snapped to the groom, already reaching for the reins. "Now!"

Within moments, I was mounted, heels pressing hard into my horse's flanks as I turned him toward the road. The Hartwood Estate. It was the only place she would be. Please God, let me not be too late.

The hedgerows blurred as I took the road at a hard pace, my mind filled with a single, dreadful hope: That the groundskeeper she had trusted was not Antonio Rodriguez.

Chapter Thirteen:

Forgiveness

I looked around frantically for any sign of a potential rescue, but there was none. The commonly travelled road was a symbol of desolation this evening. I fought against Antonio's grip, but the more I struggled, the harder his grip became. Panic coursed through me, and it seemed as though every effort I exerted against him was in vain.

"Please," he beseeched, "do not make this harder. I do not wish to hurt you, Bridget."

"Then you must let me go!" I demanded, my voice frantic and my eyes welling with tears.

But he did not listen. His lips pursed tightly together as he began to pull me towards a grove of trees, a place where we would be out of sight from the road. The road was fairly well-traveled, though not a soul had passed us for the entire duration of our interaction. Fear permeated the air, and I prayed for an escape to present itself, but around us, everything seemed quiet and still.

We were halfway to the grove, and I was growing weary of dragging my feet and fighting against his strength. Exhaustion filled my frame as I was about to give in to despair. I suddenly noticed, off in the distance, a speck of movement on the road. The speck grew larger and larger. Someone was approaching, and Antonio had not noticed. A hope bubbled up within me, and I mustered the energy to fight against his efforts yet again. It was imperative that this rider not only notice me, but also be brave enough to intercede.

I lifted my voice, louder than before, forcing the words into the open air, "Antonio, you must let me go! You are only making things worse for yourself. Let me go!"

The sound of hooves struck the road behind him, nearer now. Antonio stiffened as he turned to look at the sound. This rider was my chance at escape. I twisted my wrists as hard as I could and managed to claw my fingernails into one of the wounds on his hand. He grimaced, his hold loosening for a second, and I wriggled free. I began to run towards the rider frantically, but I only made it a few steps before Antonio caught hold of my arm once again, but it was too late. The stranger veered off the road straight towards us; he had seen us. As he came into view, I recognized William's unmistakably strong but slender form. The ride blew his brown hair back, and his countenance was obviously enraged. I could not believe my relief, not only was the rider going to help me, but it was him. It was William. Whether it was by chance he came this way or not, I was deeply grateful.

William did not hesitate. He reined in sharply, swung down in one fluid motion, and in that instant, I saw something in his face I had never seen before, an unrestrained wrath.

"Unhand her," he said, his voice low and commanding in a way that sent a tremor through me.

Antonio tightened his grip instinctively, stepping back.

William closed the distance in two strides.

"I said—unhand her."

He seized Antonio's arm, wrenching it away from me with a force that made me stumble backward. Before Antonio could recover, William's fist connected with his jaw. The sound of it was terrible.

Antonio staggered, then lunged forward, and the two of them crashed to the ground in a tangle of coats and limbs.

"Stop!" I cried, my voice trembled. I felt so helpless and overwhelmed.

They grappled in the dust of the lane, William striking again, Antonio shoving him back, both of them driven by something fierce and unrelenting. William's face was set in a grim determination; Antonio's in desperation.

I had never seen William fight, nor had I ever witnessed him lose the careful composure that had defined him since boyhood. But now he did not hold back. The two men rolled around in the grass and stones that made up the side of the road. The sound of fists landing with dull thuds made my stomach twist.

"Please!" I entreated, my voice hoarse from all the yelling, "William, please do stop! You'll get hurt!"

The brawl only continued. Antonio was a loose cannon; not only was he broader and larger, but there was no telling what he would do to William if given the chance. William being injured because of me was a thought I could not bear.

"Please!" I cried again, stepping closer despite my fear. "William!"

William dared a look in my direction for a mere moment, which gave Antonio just enough time to throw a massive punch to his face. William fell to the ground, struggling to return to his feet. I rushed to his side as Antonio sped to William's horse and mounted it, escaping as fast as he possibly could towards Ashcombe and, no doubt, onward to his home in Spain.

"He's… he's getting… away," William said as he spat out a mouthful of blood.

I stared down the road as Antonio raced off down it, the sky beginning to turn an orange-ish pink from the day's end.

"Let him go," I said mournfully. While I did not wish for him to get away with murdering my father, and for almost dragging me down along with him, I knew bringing him to justice with the law would also implicate and expose Augustus, and potentially William as well.

"Let him bid his father one last farewell, for it is something I wish greatly that I could have done myself," I implored.

"Bridget," William addressed me as he sat back up a moment later, regaining his composure after the wrestle, "I must tell you how terribly sorry I am for how terribly stupid I have been. I thought keeping you in the dark would keep you safe. But I should have known well enough that if you wouldn't find the truth from me, you would find it another way, and I endangered you more than I care to admit."

"William, please, you're hurt, this is hardly the time…" I said as I pressed some cloth from my skirt to a cut on his bleeding forehead.

"No, Bridget, it is true, and I cannot waste another minute in agony. These past several months have been an absolute torment. You must hear me."

His deep brown eyes were so earnest, I nodded my head yes. He spat out more blood, pushed his hair back from his face, and explained.

"Months ago, Father decided it was prudent to educate me on his smuggling business with your father, in hopes of allowing me a portion of the business itself. I was appalled at this. I wanted no part of it, yet I felt uneasy, unsure who my father was at this point and whether it would be dangerous to go against him. So I played the part, letting him begin to train me, detesting every minute of it. I kept making excuses whenever he wanted to work together, but I feared I was becoming too obvious. I felt a tension growing within him. The last thing I wanted was to drag you into all of that. I would rather you despise me for silence," he said quietly, "than endanger you with truth. Oh, please do forgive me."

I felt a wave of relief wash over me. He was still the same honest, dependable, and ever-protecting man I had always known. "Of course, William, you have no idea how much I've missed you these many months," I said as I held one of his cheeks in my hand.

The wind stirred faintly between us, lifting the edge of my skirts and blowing my hair around slightly.

"You should not have faced him alone," William added, his voice roughened from exertion. "If anything had happened—"

"Yes, something did happen," I interrupted gently. "But you came."

He met my gaze fully then.

"I will always come," he said simply.

The words settled deep within me. A tranquility fell between us—not awkward, not strained—but a moment charged with something long waiting to be spoken. The door that had closed the day of Father's funeral seemed to crack open once more.

"Bridget," he began, his tone gentle, "the distance I recently put between us has not diminished my feelings for you, what I have felt for you for quite some time now. I have felt an immense care for you since we were children, but, as time has passed, those feelings have altered into something more profound, and recent events have only caused my intentions to become clearer."

Despite the dust, despite the chaos of the last hour, I felt my breath catch. He kindly grabbed my hands with his.

"I do not wish merely to protect you," he continued. "I wish to stand beside you and never to leave you again."

His voice steadied.

"I wish to wed you if you will have me. Not out of necessity. Not out of convenience. But because I cannot imagine my life without you in it. I love you, Bridget, I believe that I always have, and whether or not you will have me, I know that I always will."

The world seemed to narrow to the space between us. All the fear. All the anger. All the doubt suddenly seemed to fall away.

"Yes," I said, before caution even had a chance to change my mind. "You have no idea how long I've wished for you to ask me that."

We embraced, and I felt a warmth spread through me that no confusion, no grief, no despair could possibly extinguish.

Chapter Fourteen:

Unburdened

The mirror held a reflection of myself that I would have scarcely recognized a mere four months ago. So much has happened, so much has changed, that I feel like a completely different person. Mother sat nearby and observed as Jane was fiddling with the lovely white flowers that ornamented my hair. She had been assisting me all morning, and though if it had been up to me, I would not have gone to such lengths with my appearance, I was quite pleased and grateful for the outcome. I felt beautiful.

Jane attempted to hide a tear as she stepped back and said, "There, what do you think?"

I rose from my chair and turned towards Mother, being careful not to let the pale lace of my gown catch on anything.

Mother's expression was one of great pride, and a solitary tear fell from her eye as she smiled approvingly. The events of the past several months had weighed heavily on her, though today she seemed lighter, at peace. She arose from her seat and held my hands out so she could examine me in full.

"Your father would have wanted this," she said softly at last, as she surprisingly untucked the curl from my hair and let it fall across my forehead. Her act of acceptance struck me more than I expected. However, I did not know if her words were true. How could

I? Father was gone, and I did not know what he would have wanted, in the end. But I knew this—standing there, dressed in white, the house filled with the quiet hum of preparation—that I was stepping forward into a life of my own choosing. Not one shaped by desperation or secrecy, but by honesty and love.

Outside, the carriage waited to take us to the church. The small stone chapel near Hartwood had been adorned simply yet elegantly, at Aunt Charlotte's insistence. White flowers were displayed at the altar, greenery along the pews, nothing too ostentatious, for I was not an ostentatious woman. The county had watched enough of our sorrows; today was not for spectacle, but for new beginnings.

When I stepped inside, the hush settled over me at once. Friends and familiar faces filled the pews. The Finch family was near the front, their expressions warm and approving. Cousin Rupert stood near the front as well, awkward as ever in his formal coat but determinedly present. Aunt Charlotte shone with quiet satisfaction in tears.

And at the far end, waiting, stood William. He was facing me, eyes aglow with admiration and peace. It felt as if nothing else mattered except he and I in this moment. His certainty only added to my own, and I could barely maintain my slow and steady pace. I have known William all my life, and I think, looking back, I have always loved him. I love the boy who saved me and took the blame for my accidental mistakes. I love the young man who had written me countless letters about the smallest of trifles. And here, looking at him now, beholding this courageous and kind gentleman, I feel as if it is not possible for anyone to love anyone more than I do him.

As I reached the altar, he offered his hand and gave me a happy, knowing grin. I returned the smile, feeling a surge of hope and relief. I finally felt no fear of what lay ahead, as if a weight had lifted from my heart. I felt totally free from the poor decisions of my father, from Antonio's horrid decision to end Father's life. Even though we would not live a grand life, I felt completely and entirely unburdened.

The celebration that followed was held at Hartwood, and we all found a place in the long dining room Aunt Charlotte favored for its warmth and grandeur. William and I sat side by side, still faintly dazed by the ceremony, our hands finding one another again and again as though to reassure ourselves this was real and that the day had not been imagined.

A small clink of glass brought a quiet to the crowded table, and Wallace rose, his glass in hand.

"Well," he began, a mischievous grin crossed his face, "I suppose it was only a matter of time. The rest of us have been wondering what's taken you so long, William!"

Laughter filled the room.

Wallace cleared his throat and continued, "I have known William since boyhood," and never have I seen him so determined, nor so thoroughly undone, as when Miss Hartwood was concerned. You complete him, Bridget. That alone is reason enough to celebrate." He raised his glass. "To the new Mr. and Mrs. Finch! May your love and friendship with one another carry you through with happiness for the rest of your life."

Glasses lifted, voices echoed the toast.

William's mother rose next, her expression gentle, her composure elegant as ever.

"My son has always been a careful man," she said, her gaze resting on William with quiet affection. "Thoughtful, sometimes to a fault. But in Bridget, he has found not only love, but courage—the sort that demands honesty and insists upon it. I could not have chosen a finer wife for him myself, nor a more fitting partner for him."

She turned to me then, and there was warmth in her eyes I would never forget.

"You are welcome in our family," she said simply.

I felt my throat tighten as I inclined my head.

Then Aunt Charlotte stood. She did not raise her voice, yet it carried easily, rich with feeling and authority.

"This past year," she began, "has asked much of us. Of Bridget. Of Rosamund. Of this entire family." Her gaze softened as it moved to Mother.

"With James's passing, they lost more than a husband and father. They lost security and stability. They lost the only home Bridget has known. But Ashcombe Park was not merely a house; it was their foundation. To know that it would pass into unknown hands under the burden of great debt was a shocking cruelty to follow the loss of our James."

A quiet emanated across the dining hall, as the despair of his death was contemplated once again.

"James, may God bless him, was an unwise steward of all he had, and it has become common knowledge that he left little beyond his accumulated debts, losing his entire inheritance to his poor taste in habits. For these months since his passing, Rosamund and Bridget have been required to move forward, and I had fully expected to welcome them onto our lovely estate indefinitely. That was, until I received a letter."

She paused, then allowed a faint smile to cross her mouth. There was a small moment of muttering as people speculated what she would say next.

"The letter was anonymous," she clarified. "It stated simply that all debts towards Ashcombe Park had been settled in full by a wealthy benefactor who wished no recognition, but to simply inform me that the previous heir of Ashcombe Park had given it up, not wanting to inherit something riddled with debt and ruin, and that the house was now for sale. The writer of the letter seemed to think I would have an interest in the property due to my familial ties with the previous owners."

My heart stilled. William's hand tightened around mine as I noticed him glance at his father. Augustus gave him a subtle wink. From what William had told me, Augustus must have used his untouched smuggling account to pay off the rest of my father's debts. I strained against a lump rising in my throat, attempting to force back tears.

Charlotte's eyes met ours, and something knowing passed through them.

"Rupert and I discussed it at length," she went on. "And we could think of no greater purpose for Ashcombe Park than to see it remain in the hands of those who love it most."

She lifted her glass.

"So we purchased it," she said, almost laughing. "And we gift it now, to William and Bridget. To begin their life together, not in loss, but in restoration. Not in endings, but beginnings. Not in death, but in a new life!"

For a moment, I could not believe my ears. The room erupted in astonished and congratulatory applause. Everyone was on their feet in joyful praise to Charlotte and Rupert. Mother and I hugged, and Colin gave William a friendly slap on the shoulder. Everyone was raising their glasses to us, and the thought of returning to my beloved Ashcombe Park with William filled me with immeasurable happiness. Though Father had lost the Hartwood inheritance, our home had been restored to us. The very place William and I had practically grown up together would now be the place where William and I would build the rest of our lives together. A life that would be wonderfully, gloriously, and entirely ours.

www.ingramcontent.com/pod-product-compliance
Lightning Source LLC
LaVergne TN
LVHW040223110826
845146LV00004B/1266

* 9 7 9 8 9 9 5 4 2 6 3 0 1 *